ZITFACE

Emily Howse

MARSHALL CAVENDISH

Website: www.marshallcavendish.us/kids

This book is a work of fiction. Names, characters, places, and incidents are products of the author's imagination and are used fictitiously. Any resemblance to actual events or locales or persons, living or dead, is entirely coincidental.

Other Marshall Cavendish Offices:
Marshall Cavendish International (Asia) Private Limited, 1 New Industrial Road, Singapore 536196 • Marshall Cavendish International (Thailand) Co Ltd. 253 Asoke, 12th Flr, Sukhumvit 21 Road, Klongtoey Nua, Wattana, Bangkok 10110, Thailand • Marshall Cavendish (Malaysia) Sdn Bhd, Times Subang, Lot 46, Subang Hi-Tech Industrial Park, Batu Tiga, 40000 Shah Alam, Selangor Darul Ehsan, Malaysia

Marshall Cavendish is a trademark of Times Publishing Limited

Library of Congress Cataloging-in-Publication Data
Howse, Emily.
Zitface / by Emily Howse.
p. cm.
Summary: When a serious case of acne threatens thirteen-year-old Olivia's budding relationship with classmate J.W., as well as her career as an actress in television commercials, she must rethink the path she has been following.
ISBN 978-0-7614-5830-2
[1. Self-actualization (Psychology)—Fiction. 2. Acne—Fiction. 3. Actors and actresses—Fiction. 4. Puberty—Fiction. 5. Middle schools—Fiction. 6. Schools—Fiction. 7. Family life—California—Fiction. 8. California—Fiction.] I. Title.
PZ7.H848Zi 2011 [Fic]—dc22 2010011819

Book design by Becky Terhune
Editor: Robin Benjamin
Printed in China (E)
First edition
10 9 8 7 6 5 4 3 2 1

 Marshall Cavendish

To Mom, Dad, Trey, and Olivia,
for always encouraging me

Chapter One

A WACKY DAY

I wish looks didn't matter. If I played soccer or sang in choir or participated in any extracurricular activities like most of my friends, maybe they wouldn't matter as much. But I've never been a big jock or a joiner and I've been making TV commercials for three years, so looks matter. A lot. Not that I'm complaining—seeing my face on TV is a real thrill, but auditioning can be a little nerve-wracking.

Like today, I was auditioning for Wacky Water, a national waterslide park. Usually, I feel pretty confident about how I look, but I groaned when I woke up this morning and saw, for the first time in my life, a bright-red zit on my chin. I stared at it in the bathroom mirror. It stared right back at me.

Between afternoon classes, I put on Zit Zapper

concealer. It's this flesh-colored goo designed to hide and clean clogged pores. I got a free case of it when I shot a Zit Zapper commercial last summer, but I'd never even opened the box until today. Hopefully it was still good.

After fifth period, I headed toward the attendance office. I'm grateful that Principal Brenner tolerates my missing school sometimes, as long as I keep up with class work. Some teen actors get homeschooled, but that's not for me. One, I live for seeing my friends. Two, Mom works full time. And three, I'm not technically a dramatic actress since I've only been in commercials. I'd love to try out for a TV show or movie roles, which my agent, Eleanor, assures me will come "all in good time."

Jenna Mahoney, my BFF since the first day of first grade, waved to me in the crowded main hall. It's impossible to miss Jenna. At five feet nine inches, she's the tallest girl in eighth grade, and taller than most of the guys, too. Jenna's also striking, with her straight, jet-black bob, hazel eyes, and olive skin. I, on the other hand, am a five-foot-two-inch shorty with thick auburn hair, blue eyes, and fair skin that rarely tans.

I waved back. "Yo, Jenna!"

"Wait up, O!" she called, darting through the crowd to reach me.

One of the many things I like about Jenna is that she's always genuinely psyched to see me. When she got close I planted my hands on my hips, demanding, "Hand it over."

"Patience, my friend." Jenna jiggled her silver charm bracelet—laced with tiny trophy trinkets from various academic awards—until it slid off her wrist. Then she placed it on mine, in a time-honored tradition. Jenna lends me her lucky bracelet whenever I audition.

"Thanks." I traced the delicate chain with my finger. "I'm really going to need this."

Jenna's right eyebrow shot up. "Because?"

"Don't tell me you don't see it." I pointed to my chin.

Jenna studied my zit and gingerly stepped back. "Is it contagious?"

I couldn't help giggling. "This is serious! Mom's picking me up in five minutes. How am I supposed to ace an audition looking like this?"

"You mean, like a normal teenager?"

"Casting agents want *perfectly* normal."

"I'm sure they'll love you," Jenna told me. "And if they don't, screw 'em."

"I'm not *that* kind of actress," I deadpanned.

Now Jenna laughed. "I should hope not!"

Jenna and I joke about sex, but that's as far as it goes. We're both thirteen and innocent, sexually speaking. Neither of us are seasoned daters, but for very different reasons. Jenna, a straight As honors student, says "premature dating" could derail her plan to attend Berkeley or Stanford, become a successful environmental lawyer, and *then* meet a nice, equally successful guy and settle down. Besides acting, I don't have a grand plan.

I just haven't met a guy worth focusing on.

Jenna blew me a kiss and walked into class as I hurried into the girls' bathroom. I carefully sidestepped wet toilet paper land mines and wedged myself into an empty stall. Hillwood is a good public middle school, but the germ-ridden restrooms leave something to be desired. I traded my purple wool sweater and brown corduroys for a denim shirt, khaki shorts, and flip-flops. It's mid-March and still chilly out, but Wacky Water's a summer place and Eleanor instructed me to dress "casual." It beat dressing up, since driving into San Francisco takes about thirty minutes without traffic. I have to sit really still on the way to auditions so I don't get wrinkled.

When I walked out of the bathroom, three sixth-grade boys zooming down the hall whistled at me. "Nice legs!" a scrawny blond one yelled.

I rolled my eyes because there's no point wasting words on immature sixth graders. Thank god I'll be out of here next year! I'll be a freshman at Hillside High, which will offer a whole new world of older men. I hustled into the attendance office and saw Mom at the counter, signing me out. She greeted me with a broad grin. "You look great, honey. Ready to knock 'em dead?"

Mom looked great herself in a dusty-rose sheath dress, her chestnut hair pulled into a loose knot. She's been a real estate agent for the past year and says it's important to "dress to impress." Really, Mom should be in commercials. She's very pretty, in a natural way. We both have the same coloring except Mom's taller, with boobs. I'm still waiting on mine. Megan, my nine-year-old sister, has puppy dog brown eyes and dark, curly hair like Dad. I'd never tell Megan this, but I'm glad I take after Mom. Whenever we're at the grocery store or cleaners or pharmacy, men always notice her. But Mom doesn't notice them. She hasn't gone on a single date since she and Dad got divorced last year.

We drove from Novato, the Northern California suburb where we live, across the Golden Gate Bridge into San Francisco by two p.m. It took another ten minutes to locate the three-story office building near Fisherman's Wharf. The lobby was packed with teens and adults, all waiting to audition. Assorted women and girls double-checked their makeup as a sea of Zac Efron wannabes crowded the vending machine. Thirty-something men were scattered throughout, including one pony-tailed dude sitting cross-legged on the floor, eyes closed, meditating.

I made a beeline for the bathroom. I figure if I always pee right before an audition, I'll never have to go during one. You don't want casting agents suspecting that you have a micro-bladder. Peering into the mirror, I sighed. The spot on my chin was peeking through my makeup, so I doused it with more Zit Zapper. Walking back out, I asked Mom, "Do I look okay?"

She glanced at me and gave a thumbs-up. "Perfect!"

Right then a production assistant clutching a clipboard

marched through the lobby, reading names off a list. "Olivia Hughes . . ."

Mom squeezed my hand. "Good luck, sweetie."

". . . Jennifer Womley . . . Brett Hanson . . . Thomas Albert . . . please come this way."

The assistant led us to an elevator and up to a plush corner office, where a bearded man and a woman with steel-gray helmet hair sat gulping Red Bull front and center at a glass table. The man didn't look up, but the woman caught my eye and smiled. She had to be in her fifties and looked a bit like my grandmother, which I took as a positive sign. The man, who was a little younger, stood and stroked the bushy hair covering half of his face.

"I'm Bill Hilton, the casting director," he announced. "And this is Diane Wheeler, the marketing director of Wacky Water." A few assistants were seated at an adjoining table, but he didn't bother introducing them. "We all thank you for being here. Wacky Water, America's premier waterslide park, is launching a family campaign, so people of various ages will audition together." He glanced at a roster. "Brett and Olivia, you're obviously the cool kiddos. Thomas and Jennifer, you'll play Fun Mom and Dad."

He quickly looked us over, to make sure we seemed cool and fun, I guess, and then continued. "You'll notice there's no script, because there are no lines. The chosen family will be filmed on every slide, screaming like they're on the ride of their lives."

I couldn't believe my luck! I'm a champion screamer, from watching a million scary movies with my friends. I've even won the Hillwood Halloween Carnival screaming contest three years in a row.

For the next hour, I forgot about my zit and screamed my heart out. I screamed with Brett, Thomas, and Jennifer until they were eventually dismissed. Different people rotated in and I screamed with all of them, too.

Bill and Diane jotted down notes and occasionally whispered to each other. Seeing casting people whisper used to unnerve me, but now I'm used to it. Finally, Bill pointed to me. "Olivia Hughes, you have a strong set of lungs on you. And you're very expressive! Thanks for being here. We'll be making a decision soon."

Walking out, I smiled big and said, "I was just warming up!" Bill and Diane chuckled, the way I hoped they would. If you don't make an impression in auditions, you're toast. I glided down the hall, into the elevator, and out to the lobby, now half empty and littered with water bottles. Mom set down her paperback murder mystery when she saw me. Reading is her favorite way to de-stress. "How'd it go?"

She sounded all casual, but I knew better. Mom brags to everyone—parents, coworkers, grocery baggers—when I'm in a commercial, which is really embarrassing when I'm standing right there. Dad's always been more tight-lipped about my acting because he's not a big talker and hates my missing even a nanosecond of school. He believes in a "strong work ethic," but so do I! He just means slaving away at a boring corporate law firm. Now Dad works and lives in New Mexico with his new girlfriend, Kim, which is fine by me.

"I screamed my butt off," I told Mom. "Do you have a cough drop?"

She fished a cherry one out of her purse. "Well, it beats running laps, right?"

Mom's not kidding. When I shot a regional Golly Sporting Goods spot last year, I had to jog repeatedly around a track, then lift arm weights in ninety-five degree weather. I was *thisclose* to passing out. Today the weather was cold and foggy, San Francisco-style. As we left the building I shivered in my short-sleeved shirt and shorts. I shook my arms and legs and then rubbed my face to jump-start circulation.

Mom frowned at me. "Is that red ink on your chin?"

I'd rubbed my makeup right off. "It's a pimple."

"That's odd. You never break out." She slung her arm around my shoulders. "Let's find a warm cafe where you can change and order some hot chocolate. I want to hear everything."

A rush of pure adrenaline surged through me. Auditioning can get old, but I usually manage to block out the casting agents and get into the "role" I'm trying out for. I love acting, even if it's for a thirty-second commercial. And it's pretty cool getting paid to be on TV, considering the chump change my friends earn babysitting hyperactive kids. The only truly bad part is bombing an audition. Some days you're just off—I read for a diet soda spot last month and when the carbonation went up my nose, I coughed, accidentally drooling soda. I knew there was no way I'd get a callback. This time, I felt tingly inside, the way I do when I sense that something good's about to happen. I didn't want to jinx myself . . . but I had a feeling.

Chapter Two

GIRL TALK

When Mom and I got home, it was late afternoon. Home now is a 1,200-square-foot, three-bedroom townhouse in a Spanish stucco complex. We moved here last spring when my parents' divorce was finalized. I thought I'd miss our house—an old, large Tudor on a quiet road—but the condo is closer to town, and roomy yet cozy, with all three bedrooms upstairs. I love having a view of Mount Tamalpais from my bedroom window, and I love living in Novato, which is a good thing since I've lived here all my life. It's not breathtaking like San Francisco, but it's a close-knit community with rolling hills and friendly people.

As we pulled into the driveway, Megan ran up to us, tripping over her jean overalls, dark corkscrew curls swatting her face. Breathless, she asked, "Do you think you got it?"

I stepped out of the car and patted Megan's head. Humoring her, I said, "What do *you* think?"

After correctly predicting my last three auditions, Megan is convinced she possesses ESP. She closed her eyes and began humming. "I'm getting a strong vibe."

"You're getting loopy," Mom said, opening the front door. She doesn't believe in the supernatural. "Is Barb inside?"

Barb is Mom's younger sister, but she's more like my hip older sister who likes to hang out. She's single and lives in a small downtown Novato loft, so she comes over a lot.

Megan nodded. "She's making pasta Bolognese for dinner."

"God bless Barb," Mom replied, licking her lips in anticipation. Mom's good at lots of things, but cooking isn't one of them.

I followed the smell of chopped garlic into the kitchen, where Barb was stirring tomato sauce bubbling in a pot on the stainless steel stove. Barb's training to be a chef, so she's always preparing tasty meals for us. Cooking is her latest career. She was a hairstylist in San Diego after college, then a flight attendant in L.A. during her twenties. Barb moved back here last year after breaking up with her struggling musician boyfriend. Barb has a thing for musicians, which Mom says is the reason she's still single. But Barb has no problem getting dates. Guys dig her because she's a funny, flirty, dirty-blonde babe. Except her hair's usually in braids and she wears T-shirts, ripped jeans, and Converse sneakers. You'd never guess she's thirty-three.

Seeing me, Barb said, "It's my favorite guinea pig! Here . . . taste this." She held up a wooden spoon. Pasta sauce splattered her blue shirt, which had the word BELIEVE etched in sparkly cursive letters.

I swallowed a mouthful of tomatoes, olive oil, onions, and garlic. "Absolutely divine."

"That's what I thought." Barb leaned against the granite island counter, looking pleased with herself. "We're also having Gorgonzola salad, garlic bread, and mouthwatering tiramisu for dessert. Man, I rock as a chef."

"And how," I agreed, pulling a bottle of grape juice from the fridge. I don't have a major sweet tooth, but I'm a grape juice junkie. I could swig it all day. Mom won't let me because she says it's full of sugar.

"So . . ." Barb lowered the stove heat to simmer. "Did you blow the competition away?"

I paused for dramatic effect. "Perhaps."

"You're going to be a star one day." She tweaked my nose. "Possibly even before me. We'll see what comes first—your own sitcom or my hit cooking show."

"You're on!" I high-fived her.

Now I'm not celebrity-obsessed, but I wouldn't mind being rich and famous, someday. Sometimes—especially during earth science class, when I'm bored out of my mind—I fantasize about being a great actress when I grow up. I'd make thought-provoking indie flicks, along with the occasional mainstream blockbuster to pay for my beachfront Malibu pad. Naturally, I'd grace the covers of *People* and *Vogue*, but nix the hard-partying club scene. I want to be a global do-gooder like Angelina Jolie, traveling everywhere with my gorgeous film producer boyfriend. But I'm not sure I'll ever get married, because who wants to get divorced?

We all ate dinner together in the dining room. In our old house, we used the formal dining room only for special meals. But since we have a tiny breakfast nook in our new place, we use the dining room every day. It's small but pretty—Mom painted the walls deep teal, and the centerpiece is a bundle of scented ivory candles.

Between bites, I recounted the entire audition for Barb and Megan. My voice was hoarse from all the screaming.

"Cut to the chase." Barb waved her fork in the air. "Were there any hot guys?"

Mom choked on her bread. "Good god, Barb, is that all you think about?"

"Of course!" Barb winked at me. She loves to mess with Mom.

"Olivia has more important things to do than date," Mom informed her.

"I do?" I said.

"You do," Mom chirped. "You're lucky to have a hobby that's creative *and* lucrative."

Megan scrunched her nose. "What's luc-ra-tive mean?"

Mom thought for a second. "It means Olivia does well financially making commercials. She'll be ahead when she's older."

"Ahead of *what*?" Megan pressed.

Barb shot Mom a look.

Mom hesitated. "What I mean is it's important to take care of yourself."

"Take care of yourself how?" Megan asked. Megan is the Queen of Questions. I wish it was a phase, but she's been at it for years.

"So . . ." Mom searched for the right words. "So you don't rely on a man to support you, money-wise."

"Someone like Dad?" Megan asked.

"Well, um . . ." Mom grimaced. I could tell she was sorry she'd started this. "I'm speaking generally. Everyone— male or female—has to work, in life."

Since Mom became a licensed realtor, she keeps pushing the importance of a career. Yet she never had one until a year ago. I didn't want to get into it, but Megan blurted, "*You* didn't used to work."

"True." Mom reached for her wine. "Your dad worked enough for both of us."

Megan furiously twirled her long curls. Mom hates when she does that at the dinner table. "So if you'd had a job, would Dad have stayed?"

For a second, there was dead silence. Then Mom said, "No, sweetie. That's not what I meant."

"Oh." Megan slumped in her chair. Hands down, she misses Dad the most. "But then—"

Mom hopped up from the table. "That's enough questions for tonight!"

Barb rose, too. "If you ask me, careers are way overrated. I should know—I've had three already. Now who wants dessert?"

We all raised our hands.

Later, sitting on my bed doing homework, I considered Mom's words. I agree that it's important for people to be independent—not to depend entirely on another person because people, and their feelings, can change. When I was little, Mom and Dad seemed happy enough. They talked and laughed and had regular Friday date nights. Dad worked a lot, but on the weekends we did typical family stuff like going to the park, restaurants, and movies. Then, when I turned ten, Dad made partner at the law firm. That's when he started spending even more time at the office, and less at home with us.

That same year, Mom and I were Christmas shopping at the mall when a pudgy, middle-aged woman with orange hair marched up to me in the food court and declared, *"That face could make you rich!"* I thought she was crazy until she whipped out a business card that read: *Eleanor Lindley, Commercial and Theatrical Talent Agent.* She begged us to come to her office that week, and within seventy-two hours Mom and I had signed a contract. Dad had some objections, but he was too busy working to spell them out, so he got overruled.

Since then I've been in five commercials, and I've had only a few bad experiences. I still remember one audition, during the dead of winter, when I overheard a casting agent whisper sarcastically about me, *"Could the girl BE any paler?"* Or the time I was having a bad hair day, and a catty girl reading for the same part asked me, *"Does your hair always frizz like that?"* But sometimes I get compliments like *"You're a natural beauty"* or *"What a lovely girl!"* I don't know about that, but it's nice to hear.

And then there's the money. Dad pays child support so we won't wind up on the streets, but Mom often comments that things are "tight." We've cut back—eating in, watching movies at home, and buying less stuff. Not that it's a huge sacrifice. I like that I'm contributing by earning money, even if it goes straight into my college fund. Mom says it will help a lot down the road.

The doorbell rang. It was eight p.m., a bit late for a visit. Then I heard Jenna and Wendy yapping excitedly as Mom invited them and Wendy's mom in. Well, Wendy was yapping, anyway. Jenna doesn't yap. She's low-key, and Wendy—who, next to Jenna, is my closest friend—is the opposite. They're each entertaining in their own unique way. They bounded up the stairs and burst into my room.

"The boys won the basketball game by one point. It was amazing!" Wendy executed a perfect jump in her navy-and-gold cheerleading uniform. Besides cheerleading, Wendy plays volleyball and runs track. She's always on the go and is a dead ringer for Taylor Swift, but she can't sing a note to save her life.

Jenna shook her head. "I wouldn't say *amazing.*"

"*That,*" Wendy said, crash-landing onto my purple beanbag, "is a matter of opinion." When it comes to opinions, they both have plenty.

"We won?" I said, disappointed that I'd blown off the game. I'm not really a sports fan, but when everyone goes to home games to watch, it's a lot of fun.

Jenna joined me on my antique-white poster bed, shoving multiple stuffed animals aside. They're Megan's stuffed animals, but she has so many of them that some wind up in my room.

Glancing at my wrist, Jenna asked, "So did my lucky bracelet work today?"

That got Wendy's attention. "For what?"

"The Wacky Water audition," I reminded her. "I think I did alright."

Wendy picked up a copy of *Seventeen* and flipped through it. "What did you wear?"

"A denim shirt and shorts," I replied.

Glancing over, Wendy said, "If you're going to bare skin, you need a tan."

Even though Jenna and I have explained the dangers of skin cancer, Wendy's a dedicated sun worshipper, believing completely in the magical powers of a tan.

"Why would O be tan?" Jenna said. "It's not even spring yet!"

Wendy lifted one bronzed, toned leg. "That's why there's spray tanning."

Wendy has a year-round tan and it looks good, but seems like a lot of work to me. Mom considers it a waste of time and money—she says people would kill for my creamy complexion. She's always coming after me with sunscreen.

"Can we please switch the subject?" Jenna asked. Beauty tips totally bore her.

"Certainly." Wendy dropped the magazine, eyeing me. "Guess who made the winning shot tonight?"

"Who?"

"J.W."

I knew it! J.W. Winters is the new guy—and all the talk—at school. He recently moved to Novato and started at Hillwood after winter break. No one knows what his initials stand for—it's a big mystery. Frankly, J.W. is a mystery, too. I don't have any classes with him, and we haven't had any in-depth conversations. All I know is that J.W. has shaggy dark hair, intense blue eyes, and a killer smile.

"So he's a jock *and* a hottie?" I said.

Jenna yawned. Guys, no matter how hot, don't impress her.

Wendy swatted Jenna with a throw pillow. "You should have seen it, Olivia. It was like *High School Musical*, without the dancing. We literally won the game at the last second. The time clock buzzed and the crowd went wild! Then J.W. came off the court all sweaty and bumped right into me."

"What did he say?" I asked, holding my breath.

She tossed her honey-streaked hair. "That he was glad he did."

Wendy has all the luck.

Chapter Three

HOT TOPIC

Friday morning, I woke up to Justin Bieber blaring from my alarm clock. I never wake up before the alarm because I am not and never will be a morning person. But Megan is. She ran into my room and pounced on my bed. "Do you want bacon and eggs?"

"Yeah," I replied, still groggy. We have cereal or oatmeal most mornings, but once in a while Mom fires up the griddle. I sat up in bed, stretching and yawning.

Megan sucked in her breath. "What's *that*?"

"What's what?" I grumbled, shooing Megan away.

"That thing on your chin."

Sighing, I stumbled out of bed and stubbed my big toe on the bedpost. "Oww!" I shrieked. Limping over to the back of my door, I looked in the full-length mirror and groaned. Overnight, the pimple on my chin had morphed into a flaming-red monster.

Megan was right on my heels. "It's like a Super Zit. I've never seen one that big!"

Neither had I.

I wore a Band-Aid on my chin to school. But it didn't stop anyone from asking questions.

"What happened to you?" Wendy asked as soon as she saw me in first period.

"Spider bite," I said. It *could* be, considering that it looked more like an abnormal growth than a measly zit.

Danny and Ed—or, Dumb and Dumber, as Jenna and I call them—are the official eighth-grade clowns who sit behind Wendy and me every morning. They were eavesdropping, as usual, and started making disgusting sucking sounds. They're mildly amusing, but incredibly immature.

"Want us to suck out the venom?" Danny volunteered.

Turning around and smiling sweetly, I responded, "Want me to report you for sexual harassment?"

"You wish!" Ed chimed in, and they snorted with laughter.

Only Jenna knew the truth. Walking to health class later that morning, I touched the bandage and winced. "I can feel it growing."

She stifled a laugh. "We're talking about a little zit."

"It's not little," I protested. It throbbed beneath the

Band-Aid, like it was trying to bust out. "And it hurts!"

"Maybe it *is* a spider bite."

"I doubt it. . . ." I hadn't seen any spiders, lately.

"Or poison ivy?"

"I haven't gone camping since fifth grade."

"An allergic reaction?"

"I'm not allergic to anything."

"So it's your average, ordinary pimple," Jenna suggested. "People get them."

"Not people on TV."

The tardy bell rang as we raced into class and lunged for our seats. Ms. Green glared at us. Ms. Green is young, but she's tough. She lives for giving tardy slips. Immediately, she passed out a pop quiz alarmingly titled *STDs Kill*. The whole class snickered.

As I pulled out a pen and read the first question, a student monitor came in and handed Ms. Green a note. She examined it and then scowled at me. "Olivia, your mother's in the attendance office."

My stomach lurched. Mom only comes to school when she's taking me to an audition, and I didn't have one scheduled. What if was an emergency? What if something bad had happened to Megan or Barb?

"You'll have to make the quiz up." Ms. Green sniffed.

I grabbed the hall pass and sped down the corridor through the courtyard to the office. I braced myself to find Mom sobbing, but when I walked in she was standing there, beaming. Before I could catch my breath, Mom pulled me to a corner bench, away from the frazzled secretary checking in late students. She took my hand, her words spilling out in a rush. "Eleanor called. You got the part! The Wacky Water people said you're *perfect*."

"They already decided?" I gasped.

"Yep! Eleanor said as soon as they heard you scream, they knew you were the girl."

What can I say? Apparently watching teen slasher flicks pays.

Mom squeezed my hand tight. "According to Eleanor, this is a *major* TV campaign, with four different ads airing this summer. Some rides are being repaired, so there'll be a few shoots. They're signing you to an exclusive contract. You'll be the Wacky Water Girl!"

Wacky Water Girl had a nice, if slightly dorky, ring to it. Not to mention that this would be my first real campaign. The first commercial I made—for Fabu Beauty supply store—aired in Northern California. The next two, Golly Sporting Goods and Tasty Taco, ran throughout the southwest. Last year, I shot national spots for Zit Zapper and Power Peanut Butter, but appearing in a multi-commercial campaign was something entirely new. "When does it start?"

"We're meeting with Eleanor after school," Mom explained. "She wants to go over the contract."

"Uh-oh." I tapped my Band-Aid.

"Oh, honey, don't worry. It's not like you ever break

out." Mom checked her watch and stood up. "I have to show a house in fifteen minutes, but I wanted to tell you that I'm so proud!"

I grinned. "Thanks, Mom."

By lunchtime, I was the hot topic. As I made my way to the cafeteria, kids and teachers gave me congratulatory whacks on the back, proving that news travels at the speed of sound in middle school. But I was stumped how the word had gotten out in the first place. Wendy and Jenna jumped me in the lunch line, shouting together, "Congrats!"

"How did you guys find out?"

"I saw the attendance secretary in the hall an hour ago, and she spilled the beans," Wendy boasted. "She overheard everything you two said."

Somehow, someway, Wendy hears and knows all.

It was Pizza Day, so we bought greasy pepperoni slices and sat at our usual table of girls. Madison and Lily, my friends since elementary school, cheered, "Way to go, Olivia!"

I stood and cradled my pizza plate like it was an Oscar. "I'd like to thank the Academy. . . ."

Madison—who's on the debate team with Jenna and says what she thinks—asked, "What's with the Band-Aid?"

"Didn't you hear?" Wendy beat me to the punch. "Olivia was bitten by a black widow spider. She's lucky to be alive."

More breaking news courtesy of Wendy—no surprise, she'd added her own dramatic twist.

Sitting down, I tried to set the record straight. "I'm not sure *what* got me, really."

Madison cut me off with a flick of her wrist. "Tell us about Wacky Water. Will you be wearing a skimpy bikini?"

"I doubt it," I said. I'm not ashamed of my body, but I don't have a burning desire to show it off, either. "It's a family campaign."

"Let's hear it for family values!" Lily cried. She was adopted from China and gushes about how great her family is. She wants to be a stand-up comic, so she's always practicing jokes on us. "My brother's friends were over last night. They saw you in that peanut butter ad and were saying how hot you are."

High school guys complimenting me? I blushed. "Really?"

"Really." Lily leaned across the table, her almond-brown eyes glittering. "Will Wacky Water make you a millionaire?"

"Maybe," I teased. "But not a gazillionaire like you."

"Good." Lily grinned. Lily's family is über-rich—they own a chain of seafood restaurants—but she's down-to-earth and has a good sense of humor about it.

Wendy slurped her diet lemonade. "If you're loaded, you never know if people like you for you or for your money."

"That's kinda true." Lily shrugged, unfazed.

"Who cares?" Madison said. "I say show me the money, honey!"

Jenna wrapped her arm around me. "And we all love O."
Jenna is the best.

"Well," Wendy said, "if you guys don't mind, *I'm* off
to get some love." She stood up, dunked her drink carton
in the recycling bin, and sashayed to the guys' table across
the aisle.

Wendy has always thrived on male attention. I'm no
psychologist, but I suspect it's because her dad's a major
butthead. Her parents split up about the same time
mine did—that's when we became close. We confided our
parental woes during sleepovers, but Wendy's story was
way worse. Her dad moved out one day *without even
telling them* and had the divorce papers served via mes-
senger. Wendy, her mom, and her older brother still live
in their house, but her dad eloped with Wendy's mom's
ex-tennis doubles partner. Talk about sleazy! My dad's
no saint, but he's a decent guy. He's a workaholic, not a
womanizer, and he didn't meet his twenty-eight-year-old
girlfriend until he moved to Albuquerque.

I only flirt with guys I like, while Wendy shamelessly
works it with all of them. Sandwiched between Ed and
J.W. in the eighth-grade male inner circle, she was giggling
away, and the guys were egging her on. I have no idea why
Wendy bothers flirting with Ed—I've never considered
him stud material after catching him eating his boogers in
second grade—but J.W. is a different story.

In a heather-gray hoodie and jeans, J.W. was like a Gap
ad come to life . . . only with a drop of pizza sauce staining

his left cheek. And he was smiling at me. Two seconds later, J.W. stood up and headed toward me. Did he think I wanted him to come over? Did he even remember my name? Nervously, I clawed Jenna's leg with my nails.

"Ouch!" she howled.

In three more seconds, J.W. stood at the end of our table and then kneeled down so that we faced each other. A powerful whiff of lemony aftershave gave me goosebumps.

"Hey, Olivia." J.W. greeted me like we were old pals. "How's it going?"

So he *could* pick me out of a lineup of admiring females. Our brief conversations, so far, had occurred only in groups. What was happening now felt very different. Faking calmness, I replied, "Hey, yourself."

J.W. motioned to my chin. "You okay?"

Was he seriously concerned?

"Yeah." I absentmindedly fondled the bandage, amazed that it seemed to be working for me.

His smile widened. "You're lucky you survived a black widow bite. Those things can be deadly."

"*Oh, brother,*" Jenna mumbled. I jabbed her with my elbow.

"I heard your friends cheering for you," he continued softly. "Is it true you're posing in the *Sports Illustrated* swimsuit edition?"

"No!" I yelped. I will never understand how fast outrageous rumors spread in this place. "Totally untrue."

The lunch bell rang.

J.W. shook his head. "Too bad. I would *definitely* buy that issue." Then he rose and walked off.

Jenna, still rubbing her thigh, moaned. "Did you have to attack me?"

"Sorry, friend," I apologized, grinning. "It couldn't be helped."

"Not to burst your love bubble," Jenna said, "but he may not be the deepest guy."

When it comes to guys, Jenna can be a real buzz kill. She doesn't get that boys operate differently. Sure, they're simpler creatures, but not in a bad way. Sometimes I wish she'd just get a boyfriend already and lighten up.

Still, with the Wacky Water news and one-on-one J.W. time, I was too ecstatic to let her bring me down. Standing up, I laughed and said, "Are any of them?"

Chapter Four

ABOUT FACE

After school, Mom picked me up and we drove directly to Eleanor's office in the city. Megan went to a friend's house, which she often does on weekday afternoons since Mom's usually working and I'm busy with homework. When we got to downtown, I removed the Band-Aid from my chin and peered in the mirror to evaluate the situation. The bright-red mass looked even bigger.

"What's wrong?" Mom asked. Cautious driver that she is, Mom kept her eyes on the road and hands planted on the wheel. She looked classy in her black wool pantsuit set off with the diamond stud earrings and necklace set that Dad gave her for their fourteenth—and final—wedding anniversary.

"This thing is humongous," I said, whipping out a fresh Band-Aid.

"Huh." Mom chewed her bottom lip. "Maybe you're getting your period."

Unlike many of my friends, I hadn't had one, yet. "Do girls break out when they get periods?" I asked. If that's what happens, I could wait.

"I used to sometimes, when I was younger," Mom said.

"Great," I replied, picturing Eleanor's reaction. She's a well-known agent but can be—how do I put this?—a little scary. I was a Girl Scout when I signed with Eleanor, but she convinced me to quit, saying that I'd be too busy auditioning to hawk cookies. In sixth grade, I got my hair cut short like Jenna's, and Eleanor had a conniption, warning that I'd have to audition with extensions if I didn't grow it out. And when I considered trying out for track last spring because I wanted to play *one* sport, Eleanor pitched a fit. She said in order for her to represent me, auditioning *had* to come first. I follow her rules because I enjoy making commercials, and I do audition often. So, I cut out extracurricular activities for good.

When Eleanor's not barking instructions, she raves about my artistic potential. But *she's* the dramatic one. Mom calls Eleanor a "real character." That's one way to put it. I respect Eleanor, but I wouldn't want to be like her, running people's lives.

As we entered Eleanor's office suite in a gleaming

skyscraper, I ran straight to the bathroom to see if I'd started my period, but there wasn't a hint of it. I felt relieved *and* disappointed. I wanted to be a woman—but not a hormonal one.

Mom and I waited in the reception area for twenty minutes until we were ushered into Eleanor's office. She expects people to be on time, and then keeps them waiting. When you're successful, you can get away with that.

Standing behind her massive mahogany desk, Eleanor—who's short and squatty—was decked out from head to toe in cranberry red, like a Christmas ornament. She waved her thick arms and greeted us in a mock British accent. "Hullo, girls!"

"Hello, Eleanor!" we said back.

She came around her desk and air-kissed me. "How are you, darling?"

"Fabulous." I don't go around uttering pretentious words, but since Eleanor insists that her "talent" speak proper English, I try to sound sophisticated around her. I peeked out the seventeenth-story window as her male model secretary, Peter, rushed in bearing glasses of sparkling mineral water with lemon wedges on a crystal tray. My eyes remained glued to the panoramic view of the San Francisco Bay.

Eleanor gulped her water down, quietly belched, and then plopped down on a black leather sofa, beckoning us over. "You've pulled off a real coup, my dear."

Mom and I sat across from her on a matching sofa.

"Thanks," I replied modestly.

"I couldn't be more delighted!" Eleanor cackled, showing five silver fillings. Eleanor strives for elegance, but she doesn't fit the part. "Wacky Water wants to attract Middle America and I'm sure they will succeed brilliantly, with you as the adorably appealing teenage daughter. And guess what it pays?"

We leaned forward, drawn in by Eleanor's hypnotic gaze. She set a hefty contract on the gilded coffee table, which Mom scooped up. Mom scanned the first page, and then flipped through several more until she got to the best part. "Ten thousand dollars!" she gasped.

"As it should be." Eleanor clapped her hands together. "Wacky Water is an exclusive campaign, which means Olivia cannot audition for other parts until the fall. This extensive exposure will help establish Olivia as a recognizable face, leading to more campaigns, or possibly a role on a television show. We must be selective . . . really position Olivia in the correct way."

I sounded like furniture. But to land a TV show! I couldn't wait to act in something that lasted more than thirty seconds and didn't involve selling something. Eagerly, I asked, "Can I start acting classes and join the community theater now?"

"NO," said Eleanor. "You have a perfectly natural style, Olivia. No sense ruining it with poor direction by some schlocky amateur. I'm a firm believer in working out the kinks, getting comfortable in front of the camera before going for bigger parts. After this campaign, I'll set you up with an excellent acting coach. Trust me, my dear, your career's moving precisely the way we want it."

I hoped Eleanor was right. She abruptly rose and loomed over me, her breath warm on my face. It smelled like pickles. "What's that bandage for, darling?"

"Olivia may be getting her first period," Mom hastily responded.

I nearly died.

"That doesn't answer the question." Eleanor tapped one high-heeled foot on the floor. "Can I kindly see what's *behind* the bandage?"

There's no point in refusing Eleanor so I slowly peeled the Band-Aid back.

Her mouth dropped. "It's a pimple! And quite a large one. Do you realize the first Wacky Water shoot is in less than three weeks, Olivia?"

I gulped. "It'll be gone by then, I'm sure."

Eleanor strode purposely to her desk, jabbing the phone intercom button. "Peter, book Olivia an appointment with my niece Sheila. ASAP."

Once we were back in the car, Mom and I rested our heads against our seats. Mom looked especially beat. "Eleanor's something, huh?"

I sighed. "If by *something* you mean a total control freak, then yep."

Mom smiled wanly. "Eleanor's quirky, but she has

good instincts. And there's no harm in humoring her and having a doctor take a look."

"Not like we have a choice," I said. Eleanor would probably demand a doctor's note.

"But it's worth it, isn't it?" Mom said. I couldn't tell if she was talking to me or herself. She tapped her fingers on the steering wheel, lost in thought.

"I'm game," I surrendered, reading the business card that Peter had thrust into my hands:

Dr. Sheila Tannenbaum
Adolescent Clinical Dermatologist

I had an appointment on Monday.

Dad called early Friday night, a mild shocker since he dutifully sticks to our regularly scheduled Tuesday and Thursday phone calls, but he and Kim had returned home from vacation that morning. I knew it was him from the sound of Mom's voice when she answered the phone. She was in the kitchen scouring a casserole pan and I was sitting at the dining room table, finishing math homework so I'd be free until Monday.

"Hello?" Mom said. A moment of silence followed and then she said, "Yes, we're all fine. Let me get Olivia." No *"How was the beach?"* or *"Tell me about the Caribbean!"* Mom and Dad are civil to each other, but they have a limited script. "Olivia?" Mom padded into the dining room like a giant, puffy cotton ball in her white terrycloth robe and slippers. "Your father's on the phone."

I wasn't in the mood to talk, but I didn't have an excuse. Mom handed me the phone, kissed my forehead, and stepped out. "Hi, Dad."

"How's my girl?" He sounded unusually cheerful.

"Fine," I said. "How are you?"

"Fantastic."

Dad never ever once said he was *fantastic* when he lived with us.

"How was your cruise?"

"Even better than I expected," Dad said. "We swam with dolphins in Cozumel! Did you get our postcard?"

I closed my math notebook and doodled on the scratch paper, as if I were in class. "Not yet."

"Well, we had an amazing time. Next year, the four of us should go."

Meaning me and Megan, too. I didn't respond. Dad, in his fantastic and amazing state of mind, had conveniently forgotten that I get seasick—as in gagging sick, even after taking medicine. On a Catalina Island ferry two years ago, I barfed overboard right in front of all the other passengers. I'd rather be tortured than have that happen again.

"So . . ." He paused. "How's school?"

Dad will never be a sparkling conversationalist. "Fine."

"How are the grades this semester?"

"As and Bs . . . except a C in math. Jenna's helping me, though."

Dad breathed heavily into the phone. "I wish I was there to help."

Right.

Another awkward pause. "How's the modeling?"

Unbelievable. Dad still thinks I'm a model. For all he knows I *could* be posing in the *Sports Illustrated* swimsuit edition, or even the Victoria's Secret catalog. Masking my irritation, I announced, "I just landed a national Wacky Water TV campaign."

"Wacky Water, Wacky Water . . ." Dad echoed. "You mean that waterslide park we went to once?" His disgust was clear. Dad avoids public pools because he swears no amount of chlorine can kill the germs.

"Yeah." I picked at a hangnail. "That's the place."

"What are they making you wear?" he asked suspiciously.

Why did everyone want to know?

"A one-piece tank suit."

Mom had read it in the contract, along with a requirement that I get a "level one" light spray tan two days before each shoot. Wendy would approve.

"That's alright, I suppose," he said, not stating the obvious, as in: *Congratulations! Great job! Way to go!* "I'm sure you're thrilled. I trust that the campaign won't interfere with school? Academics come first, Olivia."

"I know, Dad. Did I mention I'll make ten thousand dollars?"

"That's before taxes," he noted. "You'd be shocked how much goes to the IRS. Anyway, you don't need to earn money, Olivia. You understand that, right? Because if you—"

"Dad," I interrupted. He loves to argue. But I didn't tell him that Mom stresses about money and her job. She wouldn't want me to. "I *like* being in commercials."

Didn't he get this by now?

He let up a bit. "Well then, I'm happy for you, honey." He cleared his throat. "Have your mom send a copy of the contract for me to review and sign. And you can tell me more when I see you."

"During spring break?" It was still a month away.

Dad's tone perked up again. "Try next week."

That got my attention. "Next *week?*"

"I'm attending a two-day legal forum in San Francisco . . . and taking my two lovely daughters to Mariano's for dinner, I hope."

"You never mentioned it."

"I wasn't positive I'd be there, until today," Dad explained. "I didn't want to say anything until I knew for sure. I'm bringing Kim. She's dying to see you girls."

When Dad moved to Albuquerque to open another branch for the law firm, Kim was his administrative assistant. Now she's his live-in girlfriend—and a certified yoga instructor. I've met Kim once, last summer at Dad's office when she took us to lunch because he was too busy. She seemed friendly enough, but very laid-back. I didn't get the feeling she'd *die* to do anything.

"Listen," Dad continued, "can you keep a secret and

not tell Megan we're coming? I'd like to surprise her."

What about me? Maybe Dad remembered that I'm not into shock tactics. The one time he and Mom threw me a surprise party for my eighth birthday, I was so startled when my friends jumped up from behind the couch that I ran out of the house. "I can keep a secret," I said. He should know that, too.

Megan burst into the room, yanking the phone away from me. "Daddy, is that you? When will I see you?"

Sooner than she thought! And maybe sooner than I'd like.

Chapter Five

SLICE OF HEAVEN

Mom knocked softly on my bedroom door Saturday afternoon when she got home from work. She'd changed into gray sweats and a Berkeley T-shirt, and with her hair slung in a high ponytail, she looked more like a grad student than a mother pushing forty.

"Happy St. Patrick's Day! This arrived." She sat down on my bed and handed me a postcard from Dad and Kim's *fantastic* cruise. He and Mom never went on a cruise because Mom gets seasick, like me. Instead they often skied at Lake Tahoe, which fits Dad's personality. He's intense when it comes to sports and loves zipping down black diamond runs. I prefer bunny slopes myself, followed by hot chocolate in a toasty-warm lodge. I couldn't envision Dad lounging on a deck sunbathing and sipping daiquiris.

Kim must be the beachy type. The front of the card pictured a teal ocean, white sand, and swaying palm trees. On the back it said:

Wish you girls were here!
Dad & Kim

"Not too original," I remarked.

Mom shrugged. She doesn't say bad *or* good things about Dad. She stays neutral, except for this past Christmas when Dad canceled our plans last minute. Megan and I were supposed to visit him, but he got stuck in a blizzard during a business trip. Mom was *not* pleased, and let him know.

"Are you excited to see your dad?" Mom asked, staring at the postcard.

"I guess," I answered. He comes into town for business sometimes, and Megan and I have visited him twice during breaks. We'd never spend summers with Dad because he works so much. Honestly, it's a relief, because what would I do there? Plus, Dad and I would run out of things to talk about fast. His interests are work, sports, and the stock market—things I don't know much about.

Mom's eyes zoomed in on me. "Do you mind that he's bringing Kim?"

"I don't know," I said. "I don't really know her."

"I wish you and Megan could have some alone time with him." She propped the postcard on my white wicker bedside table.

"So *you* mind Kim coming?" I sat up, cross-legged.

"Sort of," she said. "But at the same time, you should

get to know Kim, since she's a significant person in your father's life." If she was jealous that Dad had a significant person, it didn't show.

"Mom, do you miss being married?"

She snorted. "Where'd *that* come from?"

"I'm just curious. We've talked plenty about divorce . . . but not about you or Dad . . . remarrying."

"Hmm." Mom stared out the window. It had been rainy for days now, without a hint of sun. "I'm not sure if I want to get married again. Marriage is wonderful *and* difficult. There were times I loved being married to your father, and times I didn't. James and I started out happy, but we drifted apart over the years. We got married too young, before we really knew who we were."

"Does getting married later help?"

"I think so," Mom said. "If we'd been single longer, we might've been more ready to spend our lives together. But you can't control when and who you love."

I know Mom used to love Dad, from the little things she did. She used to watch ESPN with him after dinner, hearing about his day at work while she rubbed his back. Dad must have loved Mom, too, but it wasn't as easy to tell. He worked such long hours that when he was around, he was usually exhausted. I bet Mom wished she'd fallen in love with someone different.

"So if you fell for someone now, you might remarry?" I asked.

"I'm not even ready to date!" Mom said.

"Dad moved on. . . ."

Her tone turned sharp. "I'm all for moving on, Olivia,

but if you ask me, getting divorced and moving in with someone else in less than a year sure is moving fast."

"Maybe Dad was lonely without us."

"Hmmph," Mom responded.

"Aunt Barb could set you up."

"With musicians and surfers and bartenders!"

"What's wrong with that?"

She shook her head. "It would take too long to explain."

After Mom left, I sat there wondering what spending time with Dad and Kim would be like. What if they ignored Megan and me? What if they called each other cheesy pet names? What if they were all over each other? That would make me more nauseous than the ferry. I banished the thoughts from my head, sinking beneath my fluffy down comforter for a long winter nap. I'm pro-nap, especially on cold days when there's nothing better to do.

When I woke up, the clock said 6:30 p.m. I'd overslept, and Jenna and her mom were picking me up any minute! Jenna and I were meeting our friends in the town square, which is where we hang out most Saturday nights, rain or shine. Leaping out of bed, I threw on a hunter-green cashmere sweater—it was St. Patrick's Day, after all—brown cords, and boots, and then went into the bathroom to primp.

Yuck. I studied my reflection in the mirror. The monster pimple on my chin was fading, but two cherry-red lumps were forming on my forehead, both tender to the touch.

I reached for Zit Zapper, thankful that the restaurant we were going to would be dark.

"Olivia!" Mom hollered from downstairs. "Jenna's here!"

Smearing on peach lip gloss, I grabbed my purse and ran outside. Jenna and Mrs. Mahoney were waiting for me in the car. I slid into the backseat and breathlessly said hello.

"Were you catnapping?" Jenna teased. She knows me well.

"Kind of."

"At this hour?" Mrs. Mahoney butted in. She disapproves of laziness, which I'm pretty sure includes naps.

I didn't answer directly. "I'm awake!"

Jenna laughed. "Whatever you say, Sleepyhead. You look cute."

"So do you," I said, although *cute* wasn't the right word. Jenna looked classy and sophisticated in an emerald wool sweater, black jeans, and wedges that tacked on another two inches to her height. Sometimes I'm shocked that guys at school don't notice her, until I remember that Jenna's an extremely tall brainiac. Mom says in five years, they'll be all over her. Maybe by then Jenna will care.

Mrs. Mahoney said, "Congratulations on Wacky Water."

"Thanks."

"Jenna," she prodded, smoothing her identical black bob, "why don't you share *your* good news with Olivia?"

Mrs. Mahoney is so competitive! She constantly

compares Jenna's and my accomplishments, even though Jenna and I don't at all. Why would we? Jenna has zero interest in acting, and I have even less in debating, softball, or student council. I hate that Mrs. Mahoney thinks Jenna and I are somehow rivals.

But Jenna, as smart as she is, never seems to pick up on it. "I made the high school debate team!" she told me.

I'd forgotten that tryouts were today. We don't start high school till August, but some clubs are already being set. I knew she'd make the cut. Jenna succeeds at almost everything she tries. "Congrats! How does it feel to be an overachiever?" I said.

"You tell me," she said.

"You two should be proud of your feats," Mrs. Mahoney lectured us. "Every success counts."

Jenna humored her. "Noted."

We pulled up to Slice of Heaven, our favorite pizza place.

"I'll pick you girls up at nine-thirty on the dot," Mrs. Mahoney called after us as we hopped out. She's an event planner and does everything "on the dot."

Standing on the sidewalk after her mother drove off, Jenna grumbled, "I couldn't wait to get out of the house tonight. Mom was making me fill out academic summer camp applications. Like I don't have enough going on as it is. Sometimes she's such a nut!"

I nodded, since I think that Mrs. Mahoney is a nut most of the time. Tugging Jenna's arm, I asked, "Do I really look alright? Not abnormal in any way?"

She rubbed balm on her lips and smacked them together. "No, but you're *acting* abnormal. Oh, wait . . . I get it. Are you still freaking out over your zit? Because I can barely see it."

Good. Jenna hadn't noticed the new ones. Of course, I had hair-sprayed a long, sweeping bang across my forehead to hide them. "Are you sure?"

Jenna nodded. "I'm sure. Don't sweat it, O."

That was easy for Jenna to say. I've never seen a scratch mark on her.

We walked in together, huddling close for warmth. Slice of Heaven, like always, was packed. I love coming here—I get to see friends, and the food is delicious *and* cheap. The restaurant consists of one huge room with dim lighting, dark-wood paneling, and rows of tables draped in red-and-white checked tablecloths. Tonight, in honor of St. Patrick's Day, papier-mâché shamrocks dotted the tables. Our group—including Madison, Lily, Danny, Ed, Wendy, and J.W.—was at a long, rectangular table in the back. Wendy was sitting next to J.W., talking so excitedly that when she flipped her hair back, it landed in her minestrone soup.

Jenna squeezed into a seat next to Madison but I hung back, watching J.W. and Wendy. He dabbed her hair with a napkin as she howled with laughter. Nothing embarrasses Wendy. Then J.W. caught my eye. "Hey, Olivia! Happy St. Paddy's Day."

"You, too." I crammed myself into Wendy's chair,

saying, "Mind if we share? How come you're not wearing green?"

"Hey!" She nudged me over an inch. "Green isn't my color."

I opened my mouth, but no words came out because right then my stomach cramped so badly that I doubled over.

"Are you okay?" Wendy grabbed me by the shoulder.

"Fine, fine . . ." I straightened up, clutching my belly.

"You sure, Olivia?" J.W. asked. "You don't look too good."

Another sharp cramp shot thought me, and I gripped the wooden chair for support. Lamely, I said, "I haven't eaten much, and my stomach's growling. I'll, um, be right back."

"Are you going to be sick? Want me to go with you?" Wendy asked.

"No!" I said, a little too loudly. A few people looked up, but Jenna was deep in conversation with Madison so she didn't.

Rushing across the room, I darted into the bathroom in the back hall. I avoid going Number Two in public restrooms whenever humanly possible, but this was an emergency and—thank god—the one-stall restroom was empty. Locking myself in, I glanced down and spotted a reddish-brown blood stain on my underwear. It could only mean one thing.

I couldn't *believe* that I'd gotten my first period at Slice of Heaven on a Saturday night! I'd assumed my "passage into womanhood" would happen at home, in the privacy of my lavender-scented bathroom, with Mom on hand to provide support and a tampon—or pad, if I chickened out. I'd never imagined I'd be squatting in a tiny, dingy bathroom stall alone. I wished Jenna would check on me, but she hadn't seen what happened. I didn't want Wendy to come in. She'd tell the entire world. I considered calling Mom on her cell, but she was at the movies with Megan and Barb. Which left . . . no one.

Carefully climbing onto the toilet seat and peeking over the stall, I scanned the wall for a "feminine protection" dispenser. Of course, when I finally needed it, there wasn't one. And all I had in my purse was lip gloss, twenty bucks, my cell phone, and the house key. I had no choice but to take dramatic action. Tearing off a long strand of toilet paper, I folded it into a thick wad, and wedged it . . . down there. I so did *not* feel like a woman. I washed my hands, reapplied more makeup to even out my skin, and waddled out of the bathroom, bumping into J.W.

"All better?" he asked.

Could he tell I was officially a Woman? "All better."

At least I wasn't cramping now.

"Whew." J.W. let out a breath. "You scared me a little."

Not the effect I was hoping for.

"I had the worst stomach flu at summer camp last year," he confided, as we strolled back toward our group.

"I hurled right on the lunch table in front of everyone."

"Really?" I tried to picture J.W. puking in front of a bunch of campers. He didn't seem at all grossed out discussing icky bodily functions. It must be nice to be a guy sometimes. "What happened?"

"The guys slammed me, but the girls took care of me."

I believed that.

Instead of sitting down with our friends, J.W. steered me to an empty booth a few feet away. None of the waiters scurrying around noticed, and I checked the entrance to make sure no customers were waiting for a table. I hate when people cut in line. Luckily, no one was there.

Sitting across from me, J.W. grinned. "I was tired and almost didn't come tonight, but I'm glad I'm here."

"Me, too."

J.W.'s face was flushed. *Was he nervous?* He didn't strike me as someone who got jittery around girls, but then, I barely knew him. Maybe he was shyer than I thought. Sitting here together, I had a chance to find out. I tried to concentrate on J.W. and *not* my makeshift pad, which was creeping up the back of my underwear. I shifted in the seat, praying that I didn't stain my pants and that my zits didn't show.

"So . . ." J.W.'s knee brushed against mine. "Wendy says you're in commercials."

I wracked my brain for a brilliant comeback. "Uh-huh."

"It makes sense," he said. "You're gorgeous."

No boy has ever called me *gorgeous*. Then again, most

guys I talk to have known me since elementary school, when I was a scrawny little kid. "Thanks," I gulped. "*You could be in commercials.*"

"Nah." J.W. cracked his knuckles. "I want to be a professional tennis player."

"What about basketball?" Even though he'd been at Hillwood for less than three months, he was already a starting player.

"I like it, but tennis is my true passion."

Passion. J.W. had passion. The very thought made me woozy.

"When tennis season starts next week," J.W. continued, unwrapping a breadstick, "it would be cool if you came to some matches."

In a heartbeat! "Sure."

"I miss Santa Monica," he said. "But I'm liking Novato more and more."

A weary-looking waitress stopped at our table, moist strands of brown hair clinging to her face. "Hope you two haven't been waiting long. Here are some menus. Or are you ready to order?"

We ordered a pizza and two Cokes, and I waved to my friends, who waved back, smiling. J.W. and I ate and talked nonstop until Jenna tapped me on the shoulder. "I hate to break things up, but it's nine twenty-eight and counting."

J.W. licked Parmesan cheese off his lips. "Are you speaking in code?"

"Jenna's mom is picking us up," I explained. "They

go to church early Sunday."

"And if we're one second late, she'll freak," Jenna said.

"Can't have that," J.W. said. To me, he added, "It was fun hanging out, Olivia. See ya Monday."

"See you . . ." I carefully slid out of the booth.

As soon as we were outside in the frosty air, I cried, "I got my period!"

"Woo-hoo!" Two high school girls passing by yelled at us. They kept going, cackling hysterically.

Jenna hugged me. "Welcome to the club! Now you'll realize that periods are a major pain in the butt or . . . somewhere around there. Did you have a tampon?"

"No."

"Pad?"

"Um, no."

She paused. "*What* did you use?"

"Toilet paper."

"Ick!" she shrieked. "Could Loverboy tell?"

"No!" I shrieked back. Fat raindrops pelted us, but I didn't mind as Jenna and I ran to Mrs. Mahoney's car across the street and jumped into the backseat.

"Hi, girls," Mrs. Mahoney greeted us. "Did you have a good time?"

"Yeah," Jenna replied. Then she whispered to me, "Everyone was watching you and J.W. What did you two talk about?"

"Tennis."

"And?"

"Commercials."

"*And?*"

"We had a brief but critical conversation about stomach viruses."

Jenna threw her hands in the air. "Fascinating!"

Mrs. Mahoney hummed along to a song on the radio, pretending she wasn't eavesdropping.

"J.W.'s dad got transferred here for work," I informed Jenna. "They used to live close to the beach in Santa Monica, and he surfed and swam and played basketball *and* tennis. The guy's a total jock. I didn't let on that I'm not."

"You have your own talents, O."

"Yeah." I smirked, lowering my voice. "I'm a real whiz with toilet paper!"

We laughed so long Mrs. Mahoney had to ask, "What's so funny, girls?"

Wouldn't she like to know.

Chapter Six

DR. T

Monday I had an 8:00 a.m. appointment with Dr. Sheila Tannenbaum, so I'd miss first period. I wasn't exactly looking forward to going, but I knew I needed to do it. Overnight, a round stubborn pimple had formed on the tip of my nose, joining my twin forehead zits. And I was still having cramps. So much for womanhood.

In the plush waiting room, I tried not to stare at the other patients—three teens with their moms in assorted black leather chairs. The girls had pockmarked faces, and the guy had a humongous dark-red birthmark on his cheek. They all looked miserable and, I hated even thinking it, pretty unattractive.

After we waited almost thirty minutes, a nurse in yellow scrubs called us in. Mom and I were directed to a small, windowless examining room, where the nurse weighed me, took my temperature, and checked my blood pressure—all normal. Then Mom and I waited another ten minutes, as I read the diplomas lining the wall. Dr. Tannenbaum had graduated from Yale University and Stanford Medical School. Impressive. Still facing the wall, I said, "The doc must be a real brain."

The voice that answered wasn't my mom's. "I'll take that as a compliment."

I swung around and saw a slender woman who looked *way* too young to be a doctor. She had curly black hair and wore a white lab coat, shiny stethoscope, and Nike high-tops. Her accessories included multiple silver hoop earrings and a diamond nose stud. "You must be Olivia and Linda Hughes. I'm Sheila Tannenbaum."

I liked her immediately. Mom's jaw dropped to the floor.

Dr. Tannenbaum smiled, displaying blindingly white teeth. They had to be bleached. "I'm so sorry for the wait. Things have been crazy this morning!"

"Um . . ." Mom's eyes were fixed on the nose stud. "Thanks for seeing us on such short notice, Dr. Tannenbaum."

"Please, call me Dr. T."

"You're related to Eleanor?" I asked. It didn't seem possible.

"I am." Dr. T folded her arms, grinning. "She's my crazy aunt."

"How old are you?" I asked.

Mom nudged me. "Olivia."

"Thirty-two," Dr. T replied patiently. "But I *always* get carded."

I laughed. Mom didn't.

"So, Eleanor says you're having a little trouble with your skin. Why don't you hop up on the examining table, and I'll take a look." Dr. T adjusted an overhead portable light hanging over my face and flipped on the switch. Then she gently touched different areas of my face. "I see some problem spots developing. How old are you, Olivia?"

"Thirteen. I'll be fourteen in July."

"Any previous breakouts?"

"No."

"Have you had a menstrual period?"

"I got my first one Saturday."

"Mazel tov!"

"Excuse me?"

Dr. T laughed a warm, throaty laugh. "It means congratulations."

"Oh." I smiled back. "Thanks."

"You're welcome. Well, you're entering puberty and your body's changing, in a big way. Everyone's body produces oil, but teens typically produce extra oil. The oil mixes with dead skin cells and bacteria, which clogs your pores and causes acne."

"Acne?" I swallowed hard. That sounded worse than a breakout.

"It's *very* common," Dr. T assured me. "Most young

adults experience it, to some degree. Some have a few blemishes, some develop many more."

Mom, seated in a chair by the door, spoke up. "Our concern is that Olivia makes commercials. She just signed a contract for a national television campaign."

"Eleanor told me. Under the circumstances, we can begin treatment right away, but it takes time."

"How *much* time?" I asked.

"I wish I could say exactly," Dr. T replied. "Acne can take months or even years to go away completely. Your acne is nodular, Olivia—hard pimples right beneath the skin surface. Not *quite* as severe as cystic acne."

"Cystic?" I repeated.

She nodded. "Cystic pimples contain pus. They are deeper and more inflamed. But nodular pimples are also deep-rooted. They develop quickly, and take longer to fade. I'd like to start you on a topical gel as well as Tetracycline, an antibiotic that reduces bacteria and inflammation."

Mom frowned. "Doesn't Tetracycline discolor teeth?"

"Only in children under twelve. We'll try it for a month. If we don't see improvement, we can switch you to a stronger antibiotic, or possibly birth control pills."

"But I'm a virgin!" I exclaimed. My face burned with embarrassment.

Dr. T squeezed my shoulder. "Certain birth control pills decrease oil production. Still, antibiotics may be more effective."

"What about Accutane?" Mom asked. "I've read

that it wipes acne out."

So *that's* what Mom had been furiously Googling last night.

"Generally, yes . . . but I never start with it. Isotretinion—Accutane is the most common brand name— is a potent drug. It shuts down the body's oil glands so pimples can't form, but there are possible serious side effects."

"What about alternative treatments, like acupuncture?" Mom asked.

I cut her off. "No one's sticking me with needles."

My heart pounded and I felt short of breath, like I might hyperventilate. I hadn't felt this panicky since Mom and Dad announced they were separating. I forced myself to breathe deeply, count to ten, and exhale slowly, the way I sometimes do before auditions to calm my nerves.

"Don't worry, Olivia," Dr. T said. "We won't try anything without your permission. Anyway, there's no clinical evidence that acupuncture cures acne. Antibiotics are still the most effective treatment. We just have to experiment with the type and dosage."

I felt like a human guinea pig.

Dr. T turned to me. "Don't pick at your pimples, Olivia, no matter how tempting. The pimple will only get worse and last longer, believe me."

I believed her.

"When blemishes fade, you'll probably have scars," she

said. "We can treat them with laser resurfacing, chemical peels, or micro-dermabrasion, but first we have to get the acne under control."

"Are these scar treatments covered by insurance?" Mom asked.

"Typically, no," Dr. T answered. "Check with your insurance company. Treatments can be pricey, but, given the potential severity of Olivia's acne, we'll work something out with Eleanor. She insisted that you get star treatment."

"Great," I croaked.

Dr. T patted my back. "This may sound a bit daunting, but I want to be straight with you. Your acne could increase before it improves, but it *will* improve, in time. And there are things you can do that might help your condition."

My *condition*. Ugh. "Like what?"

"In my opinion, an unhealthy diet can worsen acne. A diet high in protein and fat stresses the digestive system, which may promote breakouts. Too much starch and sugar causes the body to produce extra insulin, which makes skin blotchy, puffy, and irritable."

Mom was busy taking notes.

"A healthy diet, regular exercise, and stress management are important," Dr. T continued. "Chronic stress can increase oil production, so it helps to relax."

My mind was reeling. I didn't feel relaxed at all.

"I know this is a lot to digest. My nurse will give you handouts and recommended products, so you don't have to memorize a thing. I see acne all the time, Olivia. It's just another challenging part of growing up."

Mom and I drove silently to school. My mind kept replaying Dr. T's words—the ones I remembered, anyway—like a crossword puzzle with too many missing letters to solve. Hesitantly, I said, "I liked Dr. T. Did you?"

"She's likable," Mom agreed. "But rather young."

"Her nose stud freaked you out, didn't it?" I *knew* that was it. For a born-and-bred Berkeley chick, Mom can be so conservative.

"It's not the most professional thing," she said, pulling into the school entrance.

"*I* could use a nose stud," I kidded, trying to lighten the mood.

"Don't even joke about it," Mom warned. "Anyway, I wouldn't mind getting a second opinion."

Like I wanted to repeat the experience! And probably with some white-haired geezer not nearly as understanding as Dr. T. "I don't want to see another doctor. My body, my choice, right?"

Mom pursed her lips in response. So she wasn't thrilled with Dr. T. Well, I wasn't thrilled about having acne, but it was *my* face.

"Let's just see how things go," Mom said.

Like we had another choice?

• • •

I trudged into school. I wasn't sick, thank god, but my breakout had taken on a whole new meaning. And I didn't want anyone to know about my "condition." I reached my locker minutes before the second period bell. Almost immediately, Jenna and Wendy descended upon me.

Wendy playfully pulled on my ponytail. "Guess what?"

I recognized that tone. It was Wendy's unmistakable *I-know-something-and-I-can't-wait-to-tell-you* voice. I prayed it was something good, because I wasn't up for more bad news. Closing my locker door, I turned toward them.

"J.W. has *mono*!" Wendy blurted, like she couldn't hold it in for one more second.

"Really?" J.W. had seemed healthy enough flirting with me Saturday night. I looked at Jenna for confirmation.

She nodded. "Danny said J.W. felt sick yesterday, and saw a doctor this morning. He might be home for two whole weeks."

Two weeks! I didn't want J.W. to be sick, either. But, on the bright side, by then my skin *could* be better.

"Did you kiss him Saturday night?" Wendy yelled. Guys and girls glanced our way. Wendy never fails to attract attention. Today she was bopping around the hall in a metallic-pink top, leopard-print leggings, and bronze ballet slippers.

"No, I didn't kiss J.W.," I said. "We were right out in the open!"

"Well, mono *is* the kissing disease." Wendy tapped her fingers to her lips. "He must have kissed someone."

Jenna thwonked Wendy lightly on the head with her history book. "Enough."

Wendy switched gears. "What happened to your face?"

Of course, that question was coming. But I wasn't going to get into it. Wendy means well, but she simply cannot keep her trap shut. For the moment, a little white lie seemed the way to go. "Remember how I got bitten by a spider? My doctor says the allergic reaction spread."

Wendy's eyes narrowed to slits. "Really? Because if you ask me—"

I shut her down. "The doctor's on top of it."

"Does this have anything to do with you being sick Saturday night?" Wendy pressed. She's a stickler for details.

"I wasn't *sick*. I got my period."

"About time," Wendy replied. "Hey . . . maybe you're allergic to puberty!"

"Funny," I said, not smiling.

"Well, I hope you recover soon." Wendy sniffed. "Because you usually have a better sense of humor!" With that she flounced off to class in a swirl of metallic sparkles.

"What's her problem?" I groaned.

Jenna linked her arm through mine, dragging me to class. "You *are* a tad testy, not to mention a big fat liar. What did the dermatologist *really* say?"

Even my best acting never fools Jenna. I paused at the water fountain, scanning the crowd and lowering my voice. "It's not good. I have acne."

Then Jenna did the oddest thing. She burst out laughing, laughing so hard that she choked and I had to whack her on the back to make her stop.

"Don't get all choked up."

"Sorry, O." Jenna sputtered some more. "You sounded so serious, I was afraid you were going to say you have skin cancer!"

"Why?" I gasped. "Do I look like I have skin cancer?"

"O . . ." Jenna shook her head. "What am I going to do with you? No, you don't look like you have cancer. I'm just glad you're okay."

"*That*," I said, going into class, "is a matter of opinion."

Chapter Seven

DINNER WITH DAD

My bad mood lingered—along with my acne—all week. I took medicine in the morning and applied some stuff called glycolic gel at night, but five pimples the size of pencil erasers popped up on each part of my face. Now I could connect the zits. As Dr. T had warned, there wasn't a quick fix, and no amount of concealer hid my acne for long. At least J.W. wasn't at school to see me. I did my best to avoid people—eating lunch in empty classrooms and speeding through the halls—but still I sensed they were watching me. I knew for sure when Lily and Madison caught up to me leaving school Thursday afternoon.

Madison got right to the point. "Where have you been hiding? We've barely seen you all week. Wendy said your allergic reaction spread."

Apparently Wendy was my official spokesperson. "Yeah, well, it'll go away."

I hoped.

Lily took a step back, her shiny black hair swinging side to side. "Your face is definitely worse. What bit you again, exactly?"

"Well . . ." I stopped. I'd never outright lied to my friends before. I knew acne was nothing to be ashamed of. But like Wendy—like everyone, really, besides Jenna—Lily and Madison can't keep secrets. When Wendy discovered her dad was having an affair, I heard it first from Madison . . . five minutes before Wendy called to tell me herself. That's why, when my parents split up ten days later, I didn't tell anyone except Jenna, until I was ready to go public. I hate to dis my own sex but, in my personal experience, girls talk.

And the guys aren't any better. Whenever anyone hooks up, breaks up, or screws up somehow, everyone hears. I'm crossing my fingers that people get a life and gossip less when they grow up.

Any news about me would even make its way to J.W. at home. So I decided it was best to act my way out of this.

Squaring my shoulders, I said, "The doctor's almost positive it was a poisonous spider. She said I'm lucky that the reaction only affected my face." Adding some truth, I said, "And it may get worse before it gets better."

Lily and Madison locked eyes, saying nothing. Then, in a stroke of perfect timing, Wendy and Jenna strolled up, and Jenna saved my butt. "O, we're going to Wendy's to study. Wanna come?"

"Sure," I said, acting all casual.

"Only if you're nice," Wendy chided, but she sounded cheerful. Wendy doesn't stay mad for long.

Linking arms with her, I said, "You have my word."

When I got home at 5:30 p.m., my brain was drained from memorizing Civil War battle dates. Mom was hunched over some papers on the tiny kitchen table, still in her work suit, wearing her tortoiseshell reading glasses and gripping a pen.

I sat down next to her. "What are you doing?"

"Paying taxes."

"Can't you do that online?"

"Call me old-fashioned, but I *like* using a pen and paper," Mom curtly replied.

Sometimes Mom seems stuck in the last century, but I kept my mouth shut because she was obviously in a foul mood.

"I didn't realize you'd be home so late from Wendy's." She removed her glasses and rubbed the bridge of her nose.

"We were studying. Her mom just dropped me off. Bad day?" Scanning the kitchen counter, I saw no signs of dinner.

Mom slumped back in the chair, kneading her neck with her fingers. "I almost closed on a house that would have been a big commission, but the couple pulled out at the last minute."

Uh-oh. "Sorry, Mom."

"That's real estate," she said, sighing. "People can change their minds last minute, and there's nothing you can do. The couple decided to go with an agent friend of theirs. They said it's nothing against me, but who knows? I may not be cut out for this business. I just needed a job, and thought this was something I could do."

She sounded really down. My stomach tightened. "Are we poor now?" I asked.

"No, honey, of course not." She paused. "We can't throw money around, but we won't go without. Dad contributes a lot, financially. You and Megan will be fine."

"What about you?"

Mom chewed on her pen. "I'm okay. I just wish I could find my dream job."

"Like interior design?" I asked. "That was your college major, right?"

"Yes, but I haven't done it in years, not since Megan was born. I should have stuck with it." Mom stood up and stretched. "That's why I encourage you making commercials, Olivia. Pursuing something you love is the key to success."

I've heard that line many times now. "Do you, um, need a loan?"

She laughed. "Your money will help pay for college, sweetie. I promise we'll be fine. Enough about me. There's been a slight change of plans. Dad's in town for that legal forum, but he can't take you to dinner tomorrow night."

I sucked in my breath. "So he's flaking out?"

"Nope. He's taking you and Megan out tonight."

Dad arrived at seven. Megan was waiting by the front door and spazzed out, screaming, *"DAAAAAD!"* Even though I was in my room getting ready, I heard her loud and clear. I grabbed the blue chenille wrap Dad sent me for Christmas and headed downstairs. We hadn't seen him since fall break.

In the foyer, Megan clung to Dad like a lost puppy.

"Down, girl," I commanded.

Dad extended his free hand, awkwardly patting my shoulder. "Hi, honey."

He looked different. His stomach paunch was gone, his brown hair was no longer flecked with gray, and he was wearing a black shirt with dark jeans and leather sandals. Kim must have given him a makeover. Dad's old wardrobe consisted of business suits and workout wear. He smelled the same, like peppermint breath mints, which he constantly chews. "Are you girls ready for a night out on the town?" he asked.

"YES!" Megan exclaimed for both of us.

"Kim's waiting for us at the restaurant," he continued. "Where's your mother? I'd like to say hello."

"Here I am." Mom stepped into the hall. She'd changed out of her suit into a sweatshirt and yoga pants—*not* dressed to impress. "How are you, James?"

"Fine." He scratched his dyed hair. "How are you?"

"Fine," she repeated. "Just fine."

Could there be a more boring conversation?

Megan, still twirling around, landed on my foot.

"Ouch!" I yelled. I felt a headache coming on.

"We'll be at Mariano's," Dad said, like Mom didn't already know. Mariano's is our favorite fancy Italian restaurant in Sausalito, on the bay. We all used to go there, when we were a family.

"You won't get them home too late, right?" Mom asked. "Since it's a school night and all."

"I'll try not to," Dad assured her. "But a special occasion calls for a special place."

"Right." Mom's voice was flat. "You guys have fun."

At Mariano's, Kim was seated at the sleek chrome bar, sipping a glass of white wine. Even in the dim glow, she stood out. Her caramel-colored hair hung in long, soft layers, and she was slim and sexy in a silver silk tank top, skinny jeans, and black leather boots, nicely color coordinating with Dad.

"Hi, girls!" She stood up and waved us over.

Dad stepped forward and nuzzled her cheek. "Hey, babe."

Please.

"Kim!" Megan gave her a bear hug.

"Hi, Kim," I said.

The hostess seated us in a corner booth, handing each of us heavy menus. Megan immediately launched into a long-winded monologue about school and friends. Dad nodded, actually listening, which was unusual since he's never shown much interest in our social lives. Once Megan gets going, she doesn't stop. While she rambled, I discreetly studied Kim. I didn't see any roots, but there was no way her hair color could be natural. It didn't match her dark-brown eyebrows or olive skin. Dad says Kim's half Cherokee, half Mexican. She's very pretty, but I wouldn't tell *her* that.

At last, Megan paused to shovel pasta in her mouth. That's when Kim turned to me. "How are *you*, Olivia?"

Yawning, I replied, "A little tired."

"You look tired," Dad agreed.

I ignored that. "Not as tired as Mom. She's working really hard."

Dad drummed his fingers on the white tablecloth. "Why are you tired?"

"Olivia's on medication," Megan blurted out. "She's hormonal."

Dad's face twisted like he'd tasted something sour. "Huh?"

I could have strangled Megan with her linguini. "I'm having some skin issues. It's no biggie. My dermatologist prescribed antibiotics."

Dad held his garlic bread in midair, dripping olive oil. "Is that why you're wearing so much makeup?"

"James," Kim murmured.

His insult stung, but I didn't let on. "I like wearing

makeup. I'm a teenager, you know."

Dad set the bread down. "Teenagers don't have *all* the answers. Why didn't your mother tell me?"

Why did he always have to say *"your mother,"* like he didn't even remember Mom's name? Gritting my teeth, I answered, "You'd have to ask her."

"Olivia." There it was—the classic disapproving Dad pause. "I'm asking *you*."

"I could suggest some homeopathic remedies," Kim piped up, "if you're interested, Olivia."

Megan wrinkled her nose. "Homo what?"

"Hom-e-o-pathic," Kim enunciated. "Natural herbal cures that treat the underlying skin issues—not merely the symptoms."

"I've got it covered," I snapped. "And, like I said, I'm seeing a doctor."

"Well, if you change your mind, we can talk about it when you and Megan come out for spring break," Kim said smoothly.

Dad draped his arm around her. "We're excited you girls are visiting. But, Olivia, will you please let me know how the next doctor visit goes?"

"Um-hmm," I mumbled. What I really wanted to say was, *Why?* When Dad and Mom were married, he didn't remember our doctors' names, let alone when we saw them. Mom always handled that stuff. Why did it suddenly matter to him now?

On the drive home, Megan yapped and my head spun.

I'd divulged *nada* about school or friends, and the only Wacky Water question Dad bothered to ask was how much school I would miss. I pretended not to hear.

When we pulled into the driveway, Kim stayed in the car and blew us a kiss as Dad escorted Megan and me to the front door. Hugging us both, he said, "I miss my girls."

Megan leaned into him. "We miss you, too."

Hot tears sprung to my eyes. I felt, like I often do after seeing Dad, totally confused—glad, mad, and sad at the same time.

I cleared my throat. "See you later."

In the den, Mom was curled up in the overstuffed armchair by the fireplace, reading another British murder mystery. Setting her book down when she saw us, she asked, "How was dinner?"

"Great!" Megan exclaimed. "Dad let me have linguini, tiramisu, *and* two Shirley Temples."

Mom groaned. Megan would probably get a stomach-ache from eating so much food. But Dad never says no to her.

"Dinner was okay," I said. "Nothing to write home about."

"How are James and Kim?" Mom asked.

"Good," Megan said. Luckily, she didn't say that Kim looked beautiful or anything stupid like that. "Kim's into homopaths."

"She's into what?" Mom asked.

"Homeopathic herbs," I corrected. "She thinks they would help my skin."

Mom rolled her eyes. "I bet Kim knows all about herbs."

Just because Mom doesn't love Dad anymore doesn't mean she likes Kim. She hasn't actually met her, but she has an opinion.

As we went upstairs, Megan tugged on my sleeve and whispered, "Why were you so grumpy with Dad?"

"Like I was the one who started it?" I hissed.

"Kind of," Megan said. "Didn't you want to see him?"

"Sure. . . ." I lied, again.

There was no point telling Megan that things aren't that easy for me and Dad. They never have been. The fact that he's my father doesn't make us close, *especially* now that he's gone. Megan doesn't expect so much from Dad. Maybe that's why they get along so well.

Chapter Eight
WACKY WORLD

J.W. stayed home sick for a second week, but texted me daily updates. He still had a sore throat and swollen glands. My "condition," which I did *not* mention, was improving as well. My pimples were shrinking to pink spots that were easier to hide. There were no new ones, so the antibiotics must have been working. It was a big relief, with the first Wacky Water shoot Monday morning.

When my cell phone rang Sunday night, I didn't bother checking Caller ID because I figured it was Eleanor with last-minute instructions, like always.

But it wasn't.

"Hey," said a deep, raspy voice.

J.W.! Too excited to sit down, I stood there in the middle of my room. "Hey, yourself," I said. "How are you feeling?"

"Good. I'm rejoining the human race tomorrow."

And I wouldn't be at school to greet him. Rats.

"I can't wait," J.W. continued. "I'm tired of being home alone."

"No one's taking care of you?" I would have happily offered my services.

"Nah. . . ." He coughed. "My parents work, so it's just me and the TV. I never realized how much crap there is on cable."

"You could read," I suggested.

He laughed. "I'm not *that* bored."

So J.W. wasn't a reader. Hmm. I love to read, but not many boys I know do.

"The worst part is that I can't play tennis for a while," he said. "I have an enlarged spleen from the mono, so I have to wait a month."

"That's awful!" I exclaimed, even though I have no clue what spleens do. I was more worried about his spleen than his tennis playing.

"It sounds worse than it is," J.W. said. "Anyway, I'm really calling to say break a leg tomorrow."

"How'd you hear about the shoot?" I hadn't said anything, in case it sounded like bragging.

"I have my sources."

"Guy sources?" I held my breath, afraid that Ed, Danny, or some other bigmouth had blabbed about my "allergy."

"Nah," he answered. "They're all too busy to bother checking on me. Wendy told me. She's been dropping off my homework."

"She has?" This was the first I'd heard of it. It wasn't like Wendy to keep things to herself, and we'd gone to Totally Tan and Starbucks together yesterday.

"Yeah, we're in the same homeroom," J.W. explained. "That's where my teachers leave assignments. Wendy's just down the street so she sticks them in the mailbox. I called to say thanks, and she gave me the 4-1-1."

So there hadn't been any face-to-face contact. Good. Not that I don't trust Wendy, exactly, but the girl can flirt. Luckily, we've never competed for guys, but then I haven't liked many, compared to her.

"I could really use a cute tutor. . . ." J.W. was saying. "How up are you on earth science?"

"Not much," I said. I wish I found math and science as easy as Jenna does. I'm not destined to be a math whiz or a rocket scientist, but I could play one on TV someday.

"I'm sure it's hard to keep up with the latest scientific advances when you're parading around in a bikini on the set," J.W. said.

I blushed at the thought of him imagining me in a bikini. "I'll be in a one-piece."

"Oh well, a guy can dream!"

The other line beeped, saving me from responding. "Can you hang on a sec?"

"I'll be right here," J.W. said.

Giddy, I clicked over, trilling, "Helloooo. . . ."

"Olivia? Eleanor here. Do you have your clothes set out for tomorrow?"

"I do."

"And you exfoliated and got the level one spray tan, as specified?"

"I did." And, I had to say, my light golden skin looked pretty good.

She kept going. "When I talked to your mother yesterday, she swore that your skin's better. No nasty new pimples, I presume?"

"Nope."

"Good girl!" Eleanor yelled into the phone and hung up.

I awoke at six the next morning, but I didn't mind. It was a sunny April day, and I felt on top of the world—my world, anyway. J.W. and I had talked until bedtime, I was starting a national commercial campaign, and my face wasn't breaking out. Thank you, Dr. T!

Mom and I arrived at the South San Francisco Wacky Water set promptly at 9:00 a.m. The park was closed, but the "extras" were starting to arrive. Some extras want to be actors, too, but some are just there for the fun of it. There were men, women, and teens in bathing suits and shorts, resembling average American families. I was in a pink cotton top, denim cutoffs, and flip-flops, but for the shoot I'd be wearing a flattering blue tank suit paid for by Wacky Water. I thought about J.W. picturing me in it, and smiled. I wondered what else he pictured!

Diane, the Wacky Water exec I'd met at the audition, signaled Mom and I over. She stood tall in a huddle of people, all business, clutching coffee in one hand and a BlackBerry in the other. "Welcome, Olivia! And Mrs., um . . ."

"Linda Hughes." My mom offered her hand, but Diane didn't have a free one to shake it.

"Nice to see you both," Diane said. "Cooperative weather we're having, hmm?"

After weeks of grayness, the sky had exploded into a bright cobalt blue, with wispy cloud slivers drifting by. It hadn't even occurred to me to worry about how we would shoot if it were raining.

"I can't wait to get splashed!" I said.

"Good, good." Diane's BlackBerry buzzed. "They're waiting for you in hair and makeup. My assistant will walk you over."

Mom squeezed my hand, and Diane's assistant—a young Indian woman overloaded with electronic gadgets—guided me inside a large white tent, where I saw my Wacky Water "family." I waved to them: Shannon, a copper-haired knockout; Brad, an older Ken-doll lookalike; and Kevin, a strawberry blond who could easily pass for my older brother. Kevin and I have crossed paths many times because he's also represented by Eleanor. He'd clearly been working out—his arms, abs, and legs were ripped. I'd been doing my usual workout routine—arm weights and walks around my neighborhood—but I had no visible muscles to show for it.

"What up?" Kevin greeted me.

I squeezed one of his biceps. "Nice."

"Thanks," he said, grinning. "Eleanor told me to beef up months ago, and what Eleanor says . . ."

". . . goes," I finished.

It was nice having Kevin here.

He showed me the craft services table, full of fruit, pastries, and muffins. He popped a grease-beaded cherry tart in his mouth, swallowing it whole. "Want one?"

"No thanks." I'd been following Dr. T's advice, cutting back on sugary, fatty food. It hadn't been as tough as I'd thought, except some days I yearned for grape juice.

Flexing his muscles, Kevin asked, "So what did Eleanor make *you* do for this role?"

I figured I could tell Kevin. "She sent me to a dermatologist."

He cocked his head. "Why?"

Yay! He couldn't tell. "Minor breakout."

"I broke out bad last year," Kevin said. "I had to get cortisone injections."

"What are those?"

"Shots injected right into your zits." He eyed a glazed donut, seized, and devoured it. "They sting, but they work."

The idea of sharp needles stabbing my face made me weak. No way could I endure that kind of torture!

A goth girl with a buzz cut and an armful of tattoos tapped me on the shoulder. "I'm Meadow. Follow me, kids."

She led us to the hair and makeup station, overflowing

with cosmetics, styling products, and fluorescent mirrors. A mascaraed bald guy took Kevin to one end while Meadow plunked me down in a swivel chair at the other. She wrapped a towel around my neck and scraped my hair back tight.

"Good hair," she remarked.

"Thanks," I said. I'm always polite to makeup artists, since they're the ones who make me look good.

Then she swabbed my face with a cleansing pad and tilted it upward, into the light. "Problem skin?"

You can't fool a makeup artist. "Sort of."

"Acne scarring is such a drag." Meadow snapped her gum, nearly cracking my eardrum. "But when I'm done with you, not a soul will know." She briskly applied foundation, saying, "Whatever you do, never, ever pick at your skin—you'll be sorry."

"So I've heard."

"Have you tried bleaching cream?"

"I'm using a prescription one," I said. "And I'm on antibiotics."

"That's key. Bad skin doesn't cut it in this industry."

True to her word, when Meadow finished, my face was smooth and dewy, as if it had never seen a zit.

"Nice work!" I gushed.

She shrugged it off. "It's my job, sweets."

Next I reported to the bald guy, who said barely three words as he flat-ironed my hair at warp speed. Then I changed into my bathing suit in the bathroom.

At last, everyone reported to the main staging area, by a huge wading pool. The director introduced himself as Roberto and quickly got things rolling, demonstrating what to do and where to move, before yelling into his megaphone, "ACTION!"

For the next five hours, we whooped it up. I emptied my mind and mentally morphed into an all-American, perfect-family teen having the time of my life at Wacky Water. TV commercials may not be the ultimate acting challenge, but you *are* playing a part. If you're worried or distracted, it shows. People don't realize that making commercials is hard work. It requires repeating the same lines and actions over and over and *over*, acting just as peppy every time.

Wacky Water was different in that we did plenty of screaming, but no talking. Shrieking was easy enough as we zipped down slides and splashed into cold water. Between takes, we huddled in towels as Meadow touched up our faces and Bald Guy brushed out our hair.

"I may have frostbite," Shannon whispered to Kevin and me, shivering as we all marched uphill for one last ride. Her firmly taped, fake boobs strained against her coral tank suit.

Examining my pruny fingers, I wailed, "I'm all shriveled."

"Talk about shriveled!" Kevin glanced at his swimming trunks as he and Brad howled together.

After the umpteenth take, Roberto the Director finally

yelled into his megaphone, "That's a wrap, folks! Good work, and see everyone back here next Monday for shoot number two!"

Tired and achy, I could have collapsed right there. But collapsing on set isn't an option, so I smiled through the pain. Shannon, Brad, and Kevin went back to the wardrobe tent, but I stayed behind, searching for Mom in the crowd. Roberto caught my eye and gave me a thumbs-up. "*Perfecto*, Olivia!" he bellowed. "With your looks, you'll bring the boys to Wacky Water in droves."

In that moment, I forgot about my dripping-wet suit, my problem skin, and any other worries. I'd filmed my first big-time national commercial . . . and *I'd nailed it.*

Chapter Nine

THE VOTES ARE IN

I was yanking my English book out of my locker Tuesday morning when someone covered my eyes with his hands . . . someone wearing strong lemony aftershave. I spun around and there was J.W. His eyelids were half-closed and his dark hair was rumpled, which made him even more irresistible.

"Do I know you?" I teased. I hadn't laid eyes on J.W. since sharing a booth at Slice of Heaven.

"You forgot me already?" J.W. clapped his hand to his chest, feigning heartbreak. "Figures. You probably met some stud on the set yesterday, huh?"

"No way!" I informed him, snapping my locker shut. Kevin was cute, but not my type.

"Good." We strolled down the crowded hall together.

"Your life's been way more exciting than mine, lately. Having mono sucked."

"How'd you get it, anyway?"

J.W. didn't skip a beat. "*Not* from kissing. I'm not the cheating type."

Did that make me his girlfriend?

The tardy bell rang, and J.W. waved good-bye as we scrambled into our homerooms. I floated to my seat, replaying his words in my head until the morning announcements—delivered by Principal Brenner over the school intercom—broke the spell.

> *Good morning, Hillwood! The votes are in, and the eighth graders have spoken! The students selected to represent their class as high school Ambassadors next year are . . . Steven Martinez and Lily Chen for Marino High, and J.W. Winters and Olivia Hughes for Hillside High. Congratulations to you all! Please see Ms. Hirsch in the counseling office today for details.*

Immediately, people started slapping me on the back, cheering, *"Yay, Olivia!"* I'd been chosen, along with J.W., to be the Hillside High School Ambassador? It seemed like a mistake, considering that I was pretty inactive when it came to school activities. I hadn't even *heard* of Ambassadors till last week, when we were asked in homeroom to nominate students. I knew Jenna wouldn't be interested—her schedule's packed. So I chose Lily and Madison for Marino, and Wendy and J.W. for Hillside. How I'd won was a mystery.

During lunch, I got a clue.

"All hail the new Ambassadors!" Madison led our lunch table in a chant as Lily and I sat down. Wendy and Jenna were MIA. Wendy was making up a science test, and Jenna was at the dentist's.

"Thank you, my loyal subjects." Lily curtsied. As volleyball captain and class vice president, she's used to winning. "You may all be seated."

Cracking open a bag of baked potato chips, I spoke up. "Can someone please tell me how I got picked? I do not feel worthy."

"What do you mean?" Madison asked. "You're the perfect class representative . . . easygoing, trustworthy, and friendly."

I sounded like a golden retriever. "I am?"

"You are," Lily assured me. "And it helps that you're not too busy with other school stuff. My sister was an Ambassador last year. You have to be at every special school event, showing visitors around. It's not hard—just time consuming."

"Huh," I responded, mulling it over. I knew what Eleanor would say about Ambassadors consuming my time: *Don't even think about it!* And she'd have a point. I already had a job that required commitment and energy, not to mention answering to Eleanor. But I was flattered that my classmates had voted for me, and liked the idea of representing Hillside High with J.W. by my side.

On cue, J.W. walked up, calling out, "Where's my Ambassador queen?"

"Right here." Madison pointed to me.

"Mind if I borrow Olivia?" he asked.

"Please . . . take her!" Lily teased.

J.W. pulled two chairs off to the side so we could sit together. "Guess we'll be spending a lot of time together next year."

I tingled all over. "Looks like it."

It was impressive that he'd been voted Ambassador after being at Hillwood for only three months. And he was even home sick the day we'd voted. He was *that* popular!

"We should celebrate." He ran his hand down my back, turning my body to molten lava.

"How?"

"Wanna see a movie Saturday night?" His eyes twinkled. "I'm going with my cousin and a friend—they're freshmen at Hillside. Fitting, huh?"

"So I'd have *three* dates?"

"Not if you bring Wendy and Jenna."

I tried to think, which was tough around J.W.'s penetrating gaze. Meeting them could work—Jenna, Wendy, and I had plans already to do something Saturday night. Meeting high school boys would be a no-brainer for Wendy, but convincing Jenna? Not so easy. "What movie are you seeing?"

"No clue," he said. "You can pick."

Whatever movie it was, it meant sitting in a dark theater next to J.W. "Count us in."

"Cool." J.W. grinned. "We can get a bite after, too. It's a triple date."

After fifth period, I stopped by the guidance office to see Ms. Hirsch. I've met with her twice—in sixth grade when I needed a schedule change, and last year when Mom and Dad were divorcing and Ms. Hirsch called me in to see how I was coping. Her office still looked the same, cozy and casual, with rust-colored walls, scattered throw pillows, and real ferns.

"Congratulations, Olivia!" Ms. Hirsch sat at her desk, munching on trail mix. "Come on in."

"Thanks." I sank into a soft, floral chair.

She set the bag down. "How does it feel to be a newly anointed freshman Ambassador?"

"Great," I replied, since I figured that's what she wanted to hear. "But it, um, sounds like a big commitment."

Ms. Hirsch nodded. "More than anything, Olivia, it's an honor. It shows that you're well regarded by your classmates, chosen to be the 'face of the class.' Ambassadors attend school-sponsored events throughout the year: Back-to-School Night, Open House, Alumni Luncheons, etcetera. At these events, you take guests on guided tours and assist them as needed. Here . . . take a look."

She handed me a blue folder that was thicker than my Wacky Water contract. Flipping through the calendar of next year's events, I gulped. "Wow. There's stuff going on every month."

Ms. Hirsch tilted her head. "Are you concerned about being able to participate?"

"Well, er . . . yes."

She leaned back in her chair. "How many extra-curricular activities are you currently involved in, Olivia?"

"Let's see . . ." I hesitated. "Um, none at the moment."

"Any sports?"

"No."

"Not even one?"

"Uh, no."

"You're in television commercials, right?"

"Right!" Now we were getting somewhere. "And I'm shooting a campaign for Wacky Water, the waterslide parks. It's an exclusive contract, but I'll start auditioning again in the fall."

"Exclusive, huh?" Ms. Hirsch said. I couldn't tell if she was impressed or not. "So acting takes up much of your time?"

"It can. I have to be available when auditions come up."

"Well, being an Ambassador is a one-year commitment, minimum," she explained, "and in the fall it's particularly time consuming. But events occur either in the evenings or on weekends, and it's a real opportunity to get involved, Olivia. Plus it will look good on college applications. University admissions officers like to see diversity."

"Diversity?"

"I mean well-rounded students," Ms. Hirsch said. "Having a few dedicated hobbies really gives you a leg up."

Sweat prickled my forehead. College was four years away! And being in commercials would pay for a big chunk of it.

"Why don't you talk it over with your parents," she advised. "How are things at home?"

"Fine." I wasn't sure how much to say. "My dad moved to Albuquerque."

"Ah. Well, you should get both their input—especially your mom's, since you must coordinate rides to and from school events." Ms. Hirsch rose, drawing the conversation to a close. "I don't want you to feel pressured, Olivia. Being an Ambassador is a role you might really enjoy, but you have to *want* to do it. Let me know soon, okay?"

Whew, I didn't have to answer right away. "Okay."

After school, Jenna saved me a seat on the bus. Some days we walk home, but it was drizzling *again*, and the bus was packed. I love rain when I'm at home curled up on the couch, but not so much when I'm outside.

Jenna moved her books, and I sat down with her. Most

of the kids were yelling—why everyone yells on the bus, I have no idea—so she raised her voice. "Congrats on making Ambassador. That's awesome, O!"

Jenna does not use the word *awesome* lightly. I decided to keep my mixed feelings to myself, avoiding a lecture. Jenna's a firm believer in civic duty.

"Thanks." I peered at her. Compared to my creased shirt, damp jeans, and frizzy hair, Jenna was neatly put together in an argyle sweater and gray pants, not one strand of hair out of place. "You didn't want to be an Ambassador, did you?"

She shook her head. "I wouldn't have time, with debate, softball, and math club. And I'll run for student council at Hillside." Jenna's been secretary the past two years. "But I should warn you, Wendy's disappointed. I saw her before sixth period, and she looked down. I bet she thought she'd get it."

Wendy did seem a more logical choice—as a cheerleader, she's well known. But I'm not sure she's always well liked. Wendy showers her friends with affection, but I've heard that some kids at school find her intimidating, even though she's never outright rude. And being a cheerleader can work against you—some people dislike cheerleaders, no matter what.

Jenna summed it up, adding, "Wendy doesn't represent the people, if you know what I mean."

"And I'm Everywoman?" I joked.

"You're nice to everyone, and you're someone girls

want to be," Jenna stated, as if it were obvious. "You've got personality, looks, an acting career, and now J.W. Yet you're still down to earth . . . so don't let it go to your head!"

"I won't. You know I don't think I'm *all that*."

"You are lovably neurotic," Jenna agreed.

"We can't all be confident brainiacs!" I playfully punched her shoulder. "But since I am lovably neurotic, *please* say yes."

Jenna frowned. "To what?"

"A weekend group outing." With Jenna, it's best to just lay things out. Beating around the bush bugs her.

"What group?" she asked.

"J.W. invited us to meet him and two of his friends at a movie Saturday night. Two *high school* guys."

"You want me to go on a blind triple date?"

I knew she'd say that. "I prefer to think of it as six people enjoying a fun, friendly evening."

Jenna didn't buy it. "Fun for whom?"

"You *could* have fun," I pointed out. "You love movies. And I could see J.W. Unless you have something against him. . . ."

"Not exactly." Jenna hesitated. "I know he's smart— he's in two of my honors classes. But sometimes he acts so juvenile, O. We had a sub in history yesterday, and J.W. and some guys kept burping when she was facing the board. They thought it was hilarious, but it was just obnoxious."

Jenna doesn't accept the biological fact that ALL guys act obnoxious sometimes. Not that I'm a leading expert on male behavior, but when it comes to guys, I know a little more than Jenna.

"Guys do like to burp," I said, diplomatically.

"Well, they shouldn't do it in class," Jenna reasoned.

This conversation wasn't going the way I wanted. Trying to appeal to her practical side, I pleaded, "I need to spend time around J.W. We don't have any classes together. I barely see him! One night is all I'm asking. Will you please, please go *for me*?"

Jenna slumped, as if resigning herself to a night of pure misery. "Okay, okay . . . for you, O, I'll go."

Chapter Ten

SEEING STARS

Maybe I was *too* eager about Saturday night, because when I woke up that morning three rosy pimples were bursting through my skin, forming a triangle pattern from my forehead to each cheek. The suckers had literally developed overnight! Since my face had cleared up last week, I'd thought—hoped—it was over. This was proof that it wasn't. I slathered the prescription gel all over, praying that it worked fast.

Aunt Barb took me to Totally Tan, and then she, Megan, and I spent the afternoon playing Monopoly. Mom was out showing homes, her typical Saturday routine. When she clomped in the front door at five-thirty, she was scowling. In a tight voice, she said, *"Hi, girls,"* and marched past us up the stairs.

Mom held it together when she and Dad split, but she's gotten way moodier since she started working. As important as Mom says a career is, hers doesn't seem too satisfying. Lately she's been working crazy hours and when I told her about Ambassadors, instead of sounding happy for me, she seemed more concerned about shuttling me to events.

As much as I wanted to see J.W., my spirits were low. Not only did I look zitty but the pimples *hurt*. Medication didn't help that.

When Mom came back down in her sweats, the four of us ate Barb's veggie chili in gloomy silence.

"Is anyone happy it's Saturday?" Barb asked, glancing at each of us.

Mom answered by taking a long sip of wine. Mom's not a big drinker, but she likes having one glass with dinner. Barb often joins in. As a chef-in-training, Barb swears by wine's antioxidant, heart-healthy benefits—red wine, especially. I'm still not allowed to have any.

"I'd stick around tonight," Barb said, "if I didn't have a hot salsa dancing date."

Mom stared into her chili. "Who's it with?"

"A restaurant manager I met in spinning class last week. He's a gourmet foodie *and* a hottie."

Sometimes Barb sounds just like my friends and me.

"Do I have to stay home?" Megan tugged at her curls. "Cindy's mom said I can come over after dinner and spend the night."

Cindy and her mom live in our complex. Megan

always wants to spend the night at Cindy's. She's an only child with a game room full of toys. We donated half of Megan's stash to charity when we moved in, since we have less room here.

"That's fine." Mom poured herself a second glass. "I've got a new mystery to read."

Barb rolled her eyes. She thinks Mom spends too much time sitting home reading.

"Maybe *I* should stay home," I volunteered.

"Why?" Mom speared a potato with her fork. "I thought you were excited about your date."

"I was, until these came along." I pointed to my bumps. The Zit Zapper concealer had worn off. It didn't work for long. Of course, I didn't realize that back when I shot the Zit Zapper commercial and didn't have a spot on me.

Barb tsk-tsked. "You'd let a few measly zits keep you home?"

"I don't want J.W. to see me like this."

"Staying home isn't the answer," Barb countered. "You want to get *closer* to J.W., right?"

"But not *too* close," Mom said.

Barb waved her off. "Keep reapplying makeup and he won't notice. And if he does, a little breakout shouldn't scare him off."

It sounded reasonable enough. "I hope you're right."

"I'm *always* right when it comes to men." Barb winked at me. "They're not hard to figure out."

"But you're still single," Megan said to her.

"By choice!" Barb flashed a radiant grin. "I'm having *way* too much fun to settle down."

Now Mom rolled her eyes. She and Barb have obviously made different "life choices." Barb isn't pining for marriage or motherhood. Not that either choice is right or wrong, but I hope someday I feel as confident about my choices as Barb does.

Wendy's mom picked up Jenna and me fifteen minutes late, because Wendy and her mom always run fifteen minutes late. By the time the three of us bought our tickets, popcorn, and drinks and walked into the theater, the previews were playing and the lights were dim. Perfect!

"Psst . . . Olivia!" J.W. waved to us from a middle row, where he was sitting by himself.

Wendy poked me. "Where are the other dudes?"

How was I supposed to know? I slid sideways down the aisle. When I reached J.W., he jokingly pulled me down onto his lap and whispered, *"Oops!"* His breath warmed my cheek—along with the rest of me.

"Hi," I whispered.

"Get a room!" Someone behind us yelled, and people laughed.

Giggling nervously, I slid off J.W.'s lap and into the seat beside him. Thank god I'd listened to Aunt Barb! Sitting next to J.W. was a thousand times better than sitting on the couch at home.

"*Where are the guys?*" Wendy hissed in my ear, louder this time.

"Running late," J.W. explained. "They're meeting us after."

I thought that was funny since Wendy's always late, but from the loud sigh she heaved, she was clearly put off. Jenna didn't say anything—she ate her popcorn and watched the screen.

J.W. held my hand during the movie, letting go briefly a few times to slurp soda or eat M&M's. Our hands became slightly sweaty, but I didn't mind. And when the guy and girl kissed at the end of the movie, J.W. squeezed my fingers tight.

Afterward, we all walked outside into the crisp April night air. The town square was lit up and packed with people of all ages walking and chatting and laughing. But I was the only one with J.W.!

He led us to a park bench where two guys sat talking. I stayed out of the glare of the street lamp overhead. For once, the last thing I needed was a spotlight.

"You bums made it," he said.

One guy, sandy haired and tall like Jenna, hopped up to greet us. The second guy, with a mop of wavy brown hair, remained seated. Next to him was a long wooden walking cane, the kind you see old people use.

"This is my friend Matt and my cousin Theo," J.W. introduced them. "Turns out they don't like romantic comedies."

"Actually, we don't like watching them with J.W.," Matt shot back. "He always tries to hold our hands." J.W. smiled at me, and I blushed.

Wendy took over. "I'm Wendy. . . . This is Olivia and Jenna." She motioned to us.

Matt turned to Jenna. "We've met before, right?"

"Um . . . I'm not sure."

He snapped his fingers. "You're on the Hillwood debate team! I heard you at last month's tournament, arguing against capital punishment in the semifinals. You were very persuasive."

"Capital what?" Wendy tapped her foot impatiently.

"The death penalty," J.W. explained.

"It's barbaric," Matt said. "And costs taxpayers more money than keeping criminals alive in prison, which is the humane thing to do."

"Exactly!" Jenna agreed, fired up. "Capital punishment should be outlawed."

"Personally," J.W. said, swinging my hand, "I think the killers should fry."

Ignoring him, Jenna asked Matt, "Didn't you speak on euthanasia? I support assisted suicide one hundred percent. If people are terminally ill and suffering, they should be allowed the dignity of deciding how to end their lives."

"Could this conversation be any more morbid?" Wendy grumbled.

"Now, I remember," Matt said to Jenna, like Wendy

hadn't spoken. "I've seen you at a few other tournaments. You're a great debater."

"Thanks!" Jenna laughed, but it came out sounding like a squeak.

"It's true," I said, thrilled to see Jenna get the recognition she deserved. "She's a debating genius."

"And how," said Matt.

Matt was flirting with her!

"Some folks call Matt the Master Debater," J.W. said, "but we call him the Masturbator."

Jenna and I gasped, but Wendy laughed.

Matt snorted. "Don't listen to J.W. We have *tons* of names for him."

"And when he gets out of control, we whack him." Theo held up the cane.

J.W. shot back, "At least I don't need it to walk!"

I couldn't tell why Theo had a cane, but from what J.W. said, it wasn't some prop. Theo didn't seem upset by J.W.'s comment. I'm constantly amazed how guys can jokingly rip each other in ways that girls consider downright cruel. I nudged J.W. to show my disapproval.

Theo noticed. "It's okay, Olivia. I'm used to his lame put-downs."

"But I say only good things about you," J.W. promised, slipping his arm around my waist. "Did you guys know Olivia's an actress?"

"You've mentioned that," Theo said.

"A few dozen times," Matt added.

"We all have our strengths." Wendy kicked a rock. "I've been named regional all-star cheerleader three years in a row. So now can we go eat?"

We ordered sandwiches from a deli takeout, then found a grassy spot to sit and talk. Inhaling his roast beef on rye, J.W. jumped up, gently pulling me to him. I dropped my half-eaten tuna sandwich.

"I want to show Olivia something," J.W. told the group. "We'll be right back."

"Su-u-u-re," Matt called behind us.

Twinkly stars beaded the jet-black sky. We quickly walked two blocks down to the park, which wasn't as well lit as the square. As soon as we strolled past the iron-gated entrance, J.W. plopped down onto a stretch of grass. I sat cross-legged next to him, and he scooted closer. My entire body vibrated—I'd never felt this physically affected by a boy. We sat there quietly, gazing at the stars. I wondered what J.W. wanted to say to me. Had he noticed my zits? Was he having second thoughts? Was he going to make a move?

Finally, J.W. spoke. "You're probably curious about my cousin."

Was that it? Relaxing, I asked, "Are you guys always like that?"

"You mean, trash-talking each other?" J.W. pulled on a blade of grass. "Yeah, but it's all in fun."

"Why does Theo have a cane?"

J.W. clasped his hands behind his neck and lay down. "He has juvenile rheumatoid arthritis. He's had it since he was ten."

"Arthritis?" I repeated. "I thought people don't get that till they're older."

"This kind is different. You get it young. It's like his body is attacking itself, wearing down his joints. Theo can walk fine some days, but when his feet hurt, using the cane helps."

"So it's painful?"

"It can be. Sometimes Theo's okay for weeks, even months. It's sort of unpredictable."

"Does he take medication?"

"Yeah," J.W. said. "He has to give himself shots."

"Wow." I couldn't imagine being brave enough to do that.

"Theo's lived with JRA for years. He could be much worse off, believe me."

"Have his joints, um, worn down?" I wasn't quite sure what that meant.

"Not too much." J.W. paused. "When Theo's not using the cane, you wouldn't know there's anything wrong. Lots of kids have total remission as they grow up. The arthritis can just go away. I bet that happens for him."

I hoped so. "You guys are tight, huh?"

"Uh-huh," J.W. said. "He's family. It's cool that we live close and get to hang out a lot more now." Lowering his voice, he added, "I told him about you."

Chills ran down my arms, and it wasn't from the breeze. "What did you say?"

J.W. propped himself up on one elbow. "That I like this gorgeous girl who's on TV, but totally real." Then he pulled me close to kiss me—a warm, soft kiss, as perfect as I'd imagined.

The only other boy I've kissed is Rich Mendes, who I liked last year until he transferred to an all-boys prep school. He used to walk me to classes and crack jokes, but he never tried anything until Wendy's holiday party, when he kissed me under the mistletoe. Unfortunately, his lips landed on my chin, and it wasn't warm or soft—more like fast and sticky. I had worried how long it would be until a boy kissed me and I *felt* it, the way I did now.

"Can I ask you a personal question?" I said.

"Sure." He kissed me again. My toes curled.

"What does J.W. stand for?"

He groaned. "You really want to know?"

"Absolutely." I wanted to learn everything about him.

J.W. sighed. "I haven't told anyone at school."

"You can tell me," I said, feeling bold. "I won't tell a soul."

"Okaaay . . . it's John Wayne."

"John Wayne? Like from the old Western movies?" I held in my laughter.

"Yep. My dad's obsessed. He's seen every movie John Wayne ever made, and wanted to pass the name on to his son. Kinda dumb, huh?"

"Not at all!" Well, it was a *little* dumb, but it wasn't J.W.'s fault. And it was sweet that he'd shared his secret with me.

"You're really cool, Olivia," he said.

Then John Wayne kissed me again, a longer, lingering, four-star blockbuster this time.

Chapter Eleven

LUCKY GIRL

Sunday, I daydreamed about J.W. when I wasn't worrying about my face. After the best night of my life, daylight had brought me down with a thud. The second Wacky Water shoot was bright and early tomorrow morning . . . and I wasn't ready for it. A fourth zit was spreading on my forehead, forming a bull's-eye. I couldn't get over how fast and furious they came on. And it wasn't just my face—pimples dotted the top of my back. They weren't too visible with my spray tan, but now I had even more to hide.

When Mom saw me in the kitchen, she promptly called Eleanor and left a voicemail. I was too embarrassed to show her my back. Eleanor had phoned Friday, and I'd reported that I was zit-free. And I *had* been then. But today was a different story, and Eleanor would freak out if she wasn't informed. All day, though, we didn't hear back from her, not even after Mom left a second message. When the phone rang after dinner, it was Jenna.

"I just talked to Matt for two hours!" she announced.

"Really?" Matt's interest had been obvious, but I was surprised he'd followed up so soon with an actual call. J.W. called me some, but he texted more. Today's message from him was: *Had a great time last night.*

"Matt and I have so much in common, O," Jenna gushed. "We both love sushi, classical music, *and* indie films."

Jenna hadn't sounded this psyched since winning the district-wide Mock Trial tournament last fall. "Sounds like you've met your soulmate."

"Maybe," she said. "And Matt says J.W. is really into you, so I'm willing to overlook his barbaric stand on capital punishment. I wish we could double-date to Spring Fling."

Spring Fling is the eighth grade-only dance held Friday night at the start of spring break. Some people bring dates, but since it's for our class, most just go with friends.

"Did you ask Matt?" I said.

"No." She sighed. "But he and J.W. talked about it, saying it would be fun if the four of us went together."

"Sounds good!"

"It won't to Wendy. Remember we're supposed to get ready at her house before? She'd kill us if we ditched her."

She would. Wendy had acted mad enough last night, and I knew why—because she wasn't the center of attention. There was no telling how upset she'd be if she got cut from the dance plans. Still, I couldn't concentrate on Spring Fling. . . . It was two weeks off. Wacky Water was first thing tomorrow.

"O?" Jenna said. "Are you there?"

"I'm here." I slumped down to the floor, leaning against my bed. "I'm just nervous about the shoot. My acne's back."

Jenna didn't answer.

"You noticed last night, huh?" I asked.

"Well, yeah," she said. "In the movie theater bathroom. Are you stressing out about something?"

"I'm stressing about having acne."

"Sorry, O," Jenna said gently. "Could the shoot be rescheduled?"

Production sets don't just shut down, but Jenna didn't know that. Groaning, I said, "I wish!"

That night, it took me forever to get to sleep. Once I did, though, I had a vivid dream about J.W. and me. We were on a tropical beach, like the one on Dad and Kim's postcard, lying side by side on white sand amid swaying palm trees and a clear teal ocean. But we only had eyes for each other. J.W. grinned at me—an intimate, knowing grin—and rubbed coconut suntan lotion into my smooth golden arm . . . long, firm strokes that made my heart flutter and my insides quiver.

"Olivia! You slept through your alarm. I thought you were getting ready . . . WAKE UP!"

I opened my eyes and saw Mom standing over me. *She* was the one rubbing my arm—shaking it, actually. I checked the clock. It was 7:45 a.m., which meant I'd have to rush.

This wasn't going to be any day at the beach.

I noticed Mom's concerned expression. "I'm still broken out, huh?"

She nodded. "A little more than yesterday."

I was afraid of that. "Has Eleanor called?"

"No, which is very odd." Mom drummed her fingers against her chin. "I'm seriously considering if we should call in sick."

Mom *really* was worried. She does not play hooky. Sighing, I said, "If we call in sick, Eleanor will be furious about *that*."

"You're right," Mom muttered. "Listen, you get dressed and grab a breakfast bar. I'll call Dr. T to see if we can get in this week."

"But what about Wacky Water?"

Mom folded her arms. "Here's what we'll do. We'll bypass the front entrance and go in the side gate next to the makeup tent. We'll try to get to the makeup artist before anyone gets to us."

"Good idea!"

"What are you guys talking about?" Megan asked. She had quietly entered the room and peered over

Mom's shoulder at me. "Wow, those zits are gross!"

I hurled a pillow at her. How was I going to get through today?

Mom and I pulled into the Wacky Water lot twenty minutes late. We scurried around the main entrance, discovered that the side gate was locked, and scaled the low fence beside the makeup tent. *Mission Impossible.* We would have made it inside if Diane hadn't been standing right there.

"Olivia? Olivia's mom? What are you two doing?" Diane asked. Then her eyes zeroed in on my skin. "Oh, my."

Last time, Diane had kindly smiled when she saw me. There wasn't a hint of sweetness in her expression now.

"Olivia, um, isn't feeling well this morning," Mom stammered.

"I see that." Diane dropped her paper coffee cup on the ground. "Olivia, follow me."

She ushered me directly to Meadow's makeup station, where she was powdering Kevin's face. Diane announced, "It's Olivia's turn."

Kevin scrambled out of the chair, shot me a confused look, and made a beeline for the pastry cart. Meadow, snapping bubble gum, eased me into the chair. Diane watched as Meadow went to work on me. I barely breathed until Meadow was done and I saw in the mirror that my "problem skin" was hidden beneath a heavy cosmetic veil. The makeup was overdone close up, but

I knew it wouldn't show in the far-range camera shots.

"It'll do," Diane said. "How long has this been going on, Olivia?"

"A few weeks." I gulped. "I'm, um, seeing a dermatologist. Eleanor recommended her."

Instantly, I regretted those last three words.

"Eleanor knows?" Diane sighed. "Well, I'll be speaking to her. Seeing your doctor is critical, Olivia. And even then . . ."

"It'll get better," I promised. What else could I say?

"Let's hope so." Diane started moving away but swiveled back, adding, "Meadow, stand by for emergency touch-ups." To me, she said, "You understand this isn't personal, Olivia? It's just business."

And I was blowing it.

Meadow patted my shoulder after she left. "Sorry, kid."

"Thanks."

Shaky and sweaty, I got into wardrobe and lumbered over to the main staging area to join my Wacky Water family. We were all dressed in short-sleeved tops and shorts because the first scene called for us to be eating in the food court.

"Brad, Shannon, Kevin, and Olivia . . . places, please!" Roberto the Director bellowed from the snack stand.

"Yes, sir!" Kevin, who can get a little hyper, broke into a run. But in his hurry, he skidded in a puddle of water, twisting his leg and landing sideways on the pavement. "My foot!" Kevin clutched his right ankle, wincing. "It hurts really bad!"

And that's how I got my lucky break.

Mom drove me to school, both of us in shock. "Poor Kevin," she said.

I was still trembling. "You mean, lucky us."

Kevin and his sprained ankle had been carted off in an ambulance. It was a precaution legally required on the set. Roberto, Diane, and a few other bigwigs huddled in conference as the rest of us actors, crew, and extras stood there, awaiting instructions.

At last, Roberto spoke into the megaphone. *"Today's shoot is canceled. Rescheduling information will be sent out shortly. Everyone dismissed!"*

I felt terrible that Kevin had gotten injured, but I must have had a guardian angel watching out for me. The only problem now was showing up at school wearing a gallon of makeup. The thick pancake foundation had hardened into a clay-like mask. If I moved one muscle, it might crack.

I arrived at school right as lunch ended and kids flooded the halls, so I waited in the attendance office until the crowd thinned. Then I rushed into English class, head down, past Lily, Madison, Wendy, Danny, and Ed to my desk in the back, praying they were too busy yapping to notice me. No such luck.

"What are you doing here?" Wendy yelled down the aisle. "I thought you were shooting at Wacky Water all day."

Burying my head in my notebook, I answered, "An actor got hurt, so the shoot was postponed."

"Is that why you're wearing all that makeup?" she asked. Loudly.

I stared at Wendy, hoping it might shut her up. Danny and Ed were smirking. Even Madison and Lily looked amused.

Wendy didn't clue in. "Seriously, Olivia, *what's on your face?*"

"Stage makeup," I said tersely. "You have to wear a ton so you don't look washed out on TV."

"You should wash it *off*," Madison suggested, joining in. "You look . . . different."

Madison isn't Miss Sensitive, either.

"Like a wax figure," Lily said playfully.

"Like your face is frozen!" Ed piled on.

Guys in the class snickered.

"It's *stage* makeup," I repeated. "For ACTING."

"Are you playing the Joker?" Danny asked. The entire class cracked up.

Tears burned my eyes.

Mr. Frankel strolled in, asking, "What's so funny?"

Me! I raised my hand, forcing my voice to remain steady. "Can I get a pass for the nurse? I feel sick."

I spent the rest of fifth period hiding in a bathroom stall. I did look like a freak, and I'd only look ten times worse without makeup! What would people say when they saw me then? What if my acne got worse? What would happen to my acting career? I hated feeling sorry for myself, but I didn't know what to do. I sat there on a toilet lid until the bell rang and Wendy and Madison walked in, chattering away like nothing had happened.

"I can't wait for Spring Fling," Madison said. "I can't believe it's our last dance here. Steve's taking me out to a fancy restaurant before."

"Fun," Wendy said. "I'm going with Jenna and Olivia. I'll tell her to go easy on the makeup!"

Traitor. Wendy was lucky we hadn't ditched her to go with J.W. and Matt. I wished we had.

"That was so weird in class," Madison said. "I know Olivia had that allergy thing, but she looked really strange. What's going on?"

I stiffened, waiting to hear Wendy's response.

"Beats me," Wendy said. "She's so moody lately. I don't know what her problem is."

Hearing Wendy say that annoyed me big time, even if her words were technically true.

They used the bathroom, and then blasted the sink to wash their hands.

"Well, J.W. seems to dig her," Madison continued. "I hope Olivia gets better, whatever's happening."

"Me, too," Wendy said.

Me, three.

They left the bathroom, and I could finally breathe.

Chapter Twelve

PAGING DR. T

I spent sixth period in the nurse's office. The nurse was out, but the office secretary took one look at me and led me to the sick room, no questions asked. Seconds later, Ms. Hirsch strolled past and saw me lying on the cot. She ducked her head in. "Everything alright, Olivia?"

"Um, yeah." I was grateful for the darkness of the room. "I just don't feel too hot."

"Sorry to hear that." Ms. Hirsch hovered in the doorway. "Is that why you haven't gotten back to me about Ambassadors?"

I'm not normally a forgetful person, but I had COMPLETELY blanked about Ambassadors! So much for school spirit. Sitting up, I said, "I'm sorry, Ms. Hirsch.

Things have been hectic."

"Not so hectic you're going to pass up being an Ambassador, I hope."

I had to hand it to Ms. Hirsch—she was one determined woman. It would be simpler to go ahead and give her an answer. Mom had said we'd work out the rides somehow. Maybe J.W. and I could carpool. "I'll do it."

"Terrific!" she cried. "Stop by my office this week and I'll give you the forms to sign. Don't forget, okay?"

"Okay." I lay back down.

"And Olivia?" she said. "If there's anything you'd like to talk about, anything at all, I'm available."

Great. Even Ms. Hirsch knew something was wrong.

When the school dismissal bell rang, I sat there an extra thirty minutes so I wouldn't run into J.W. or my friends. Then I trudged the two miles home, headed straight upstairs to my room, and dove into bed. I would have remained there a long time if Megan hadn't burst into my bedroom.

"Olivia?" Megan shook me. "Mom's waiting for you in the car."

"Why?" I groaned, pulling the covers over my head.

She yanked them off. "I don't know. But she's taking me to Cindy's."

I dragged myself out of bed and followed Megan outside to Mom's dusty black minivan.

"Where are we going?" I asked, getting in.

"Eleanor called." Mom's hands gripped the steering wheel. "And she wants to see us now."

For the first time, Eleanor didn't keep us waiting. Peter practically shoved us into her office. Eleanor stood fuming behind her mahogany desk. She was dressed in a hot-pink suit, like a giant Easter egg ready to hatch, which I would have found funny if I wasn't so scared.

Eleanor pointed for us to sit. "Well, Linda and Olivia, I can't say it's good to see you two."

Mom cleared her throat. "We've, uh, been trying to reach you."

"I was in Chicago for the birth of my first granddaughter and grandson," she said.

"Twins!" Mom exclaimed. "Congratulations!"

"They were born prematurely."

"Oh," Mom said. "I'm so—"

Eleanor cut her off. "They'll be fine. But, as you can imagine, it was a stressful weekend. I left my BlackBerry in a cab, so I didn't bother with messages. What I *did* get was an urgent call from Diane when I returned to my office this afternoon. To put it mildly, she's not pleased."

"But—" I started.

"No 'buts.' Diane's VERY concerned about the state of your skin, as am I. Excessive makeup is *not* the answer." Eleanor addressed Mom, "I thought you two were on top of this."

"We are," Mom said. "And we're seeing Dr.

Tannenbaum again on Thursday."

"Correction. I called Sheila. She's expecting you in an hour." Eleanor plopped into her chair. "Olivia, I'll be frank. I consider you a beloved protégé. You've been a reliable professional from day one, and I sympathize that you're having a rough spell. You're lucky that knucklehead Kevin injured his foot. He suffered ligament damage, and has to wear a splint. *He's* lucky the injury occurred on set. The Wacky Water execs don't want to risk a workplace lawsuit. As long as Kevin's ankle heals within a few weeks, he won't be replaced. You've been given the gift of time, Olivia, but it *cannot* be squandered."

"She's doing everything Dr. T recommended," Mom said defensively.

"It's not enough," Eleanor countered. "Sheila assured me she'll step up the treatment. This skin disorder *must* be cured."

Mom was visibly upset now. "Olivia has teen acne. It's not fatal."

"But it could be fatal to Olivia's career. She has the potential to go far, but she won't go *anywhere* the way she looks now."

I felt like a total loser. But I wouldn't bawl in front of Eleanor. I walked over to the high-rise window and stared at the tiny white sailboats drifting in the choppy bay below. I wished I was in one of them, sailing away.

• • •

Mom and I went straight from Eleanor's swanky office to Dr. T's sterile examining room. She came in and greeted me with a sympathetic smile. "I hear Eleanor's on the warpath."

"Oh, yeah," I said.

Dr. T examined my face and then pulled my paper robe down slightly, revealing my pimple-studded shoulders. "When did you first notice these?"

"You have acne on your back?" Mom's eyes widened. "Why didn't you tell me, Olivia?"

"I just didn't," I snapped. I don't have to tell Mom *everything*.

"Olivia," Dr. T kept her eyes on me, "are you using the prescription products there, too?"

I nodded.

"Good. Follow the same cleansing routine for your face, back, *and* chest, just in case. And we can try a stronger medication."

"Accutane?" Mom asked.

"I'd like to try Minocycline, another antibiotic," Dr. T said. "There are also possible side effects, but they're rare—headaches and upset stomach, mainly."

Gheesh.

"We should see improvement in a few weeks," Dr. T went on. "Though it takes several weeks to get the full effect. If it's not enough, we might consider something else. How does that sound?"

I felt torn. I wanted my acne to vanish quickly *without* side effects. "I know what Eleanor would say."

"Well, I'm your doctor," Dr. T reminded me. "And with doctor-patient confidentiality, no matter how much Eleanor pesters me, I won't tell her a thing."

"About the Wacky Water campaign," Mom broke in. "The next shoot's in a few weeks. If things aren't better . . ."

Dr. T held up her hand. "I know you're in a tough spot, guys. Having acne is difficult and being an actress makes it even harder, I'm sure. Medically, however, I'm not comfortable prescribing more medicine than needed. But I'm curious . . . is anyone besides Eleanor giving you a hard time, Olivia?"

"Kind of," I said, my voice wobbly.

Mom looked up. "Did something happen?"

"Just kids at school joking around." I didn't want to admit it was my own friends.

"Tell you what." Dr. T studied me. "Let's start Olivia on the new antibiotic today, and see how it does. In the meantime, I can offer a temporary solution. Have either of you heard of cortisone shots?"

I shuddered, recalling Kevin's graphic description. "Shots injected in pimples?"

"The technical term is corticosteroid injection," she said.

"They're *steroids*?"

"Yes, but not the kind some athletes misuse. The injected spots usually clear quickly, with less chance of scarring. It's not a permanent fix, but it could help."

"Okayyy . . ." I inhaled deeply. Man, I hate needles. And that's normally just in my arm! Mom reached for my hand.

Dr. T picked up a long, gleaming syringe, inserted it into a liquid vial, and squirted a few drops into the air. "This will sting, but I'll make it quick."

I closed my eyes as she swabbed my skin clean with a cool pad. Before I could change my mind, I felt five pricks, one after another. Each stung a little.

Then it was over.

"Sorry about that, Olivia," Dr. T said. "How about a lollipop for being such a brave patient?"

"I prefer jewelry," I weakly joked.

"That's my girl," Mom said. She didn't look so hot herself—her face was pale and damp.

Dr. T smiled. "Olivia's a trooper. There's a little blood, so my nurse will place cotton adhesives on the sites. You may not want to make any big social plans tonight."

"I'm going right home," I said.

Back in the reception area, Mom stood in line to pay for the visit. Limply, I sat down to rest. Today had been rough, in every way, from start to finish. All I wanted to do was lie on the den couch and eat Thai leftovers. Or maybe Barb was there, concocting some delicious feast. I realized I hadn't eaten since breakfast, and my stomach rumbled.

"Want a mint?" a deep voice asked.

That's when I noticed the guy sitting in the chair across from me. He was casually dressed in a navy T-shirt and baggy khakis, cute in a scruffy way, and vaguely familiar.

"Olivia, right?" he said. "I'm Theo—J.W.'s cousin."

I froze. When I met Theo that Saturday night, we were outside and I didn't get a good look at him. And now that he saw *me*, there were five bloody mini-cotton balls taped to my face.

Picking up on my hesitation, he kidded, "Bet you don't recognize me without my cane."

"Oh!" I sputtered. Nothing else came out. Theo seemed friendly, but the last thing I wanted was news of my doc visit getting back to J.W. I'd be lucky if he didn't hear about the English class incident.

"You okay?" Theo asked.

He was being polite. Clearly, I wasn't okay. "I've been better. I don't normally look like this."

"I figured that." Theo smiled. "I've seen Dr. T for years. Sometimes I get allergic rashes from medicine. Gross, huh?"

I was now officially the lowest of low. As much as my acne bothered me, Theo was dealing with a way more serious problem. I wasn't sure he knew J.W. had told me about his arthritis. Trying to make light of things, I said, "I'd settle for a rash."

"Hey!" Theo snapped his fingers. "I hear we're going to Spring Fling together."

"We are?"

"J.W. thinks we should all go: you, him, Jenna, Matt, Wendy, and me." He stopped. "And, uh, from the look on your face, guess he hasn't said anything?"

"Not exactly."

"He will. Since you're an actress and all, can you act surprised when he does?"

Smiling in spite of myself, I said, "I can do that."

Theo's words were the only encouraging ones I'd heard all day. I was going to Spring Fling as J.W.'s date after all! And Jenna would get to be with Matt. I couldn't picture Theo and Wendy together, though, since she'd acted like a brat the night we all met. But guys tend to dig Wendy whether she's bratty or not. For Theo's sake, I hoped that he didn't. I doubted Wendy would be into Theo, with his cane and everything. She always goes for jocks.

"Olivia . . ." Mom called, waiting at the door.

I stood, saying, "It was nice seeing you." And I meant it.

"You, too," Theo said. "And Olivia?"

"Yeah?"

"J.W. won't even know we were here."

"Thanks, Theo."

He mock-saluted. "Anytime."

Chapter Thirteen

SPRING FLING

Thanks to Dr. T, my pimples deflated fast. They were noticeably smaller Tuesday morning. When I arrived at school, J.W. and Ed saw me in the main hall first thing.

"What happened to your mask?" asked Ed.

"Huh?" J.W.'s eyes darted from Ed to me.

Thinking fast, I said, "Ed harassed me yesterday because I came to school from Wacky Water, wearing stage makeup."

"You were here yesterday?" J.W. looked surprised. He didn't pick up on the harassment part.

"Be glad you missed her," Ed said.

Examining my face, J.W. asked, "Are you having another allergic reaction?"

"These things?" I patted my bumps like they were no

biggie. "Yeah, guess I'm allergic to some makeup, too. I must have super-sensitive skin."

"You mean super-scary," Ed said.

J.W. ignored him. "Poor baby." He slung his arm around me and steered me down the hall, away from Ed. "How long do they last?"

"They should be gone in a few days." I prayed Dr. T's timetable was right.

"So you'll be fine by Friday!"

I knew where J.W. was going with this, but, being the experienced actress I am, I played along. "What's Friday?"

"Helloo . . . Spring Fling? Would a future star like you go with a regular dude like me?"

"I think I could handle that," I said. We stopped in the hall, holding hands. Two seventh-grade girls bumped into us, both making eyes at J.W.

"Cool." He beamed. *Had J.W. thought for one second that I'd say no?* "Sorry for asking this late, but since you and Jenna and Wendy travel in a pack, I needed a game plan. You up for another triple date?"

Sounding more confident than I felt, I said, "I'm up for anything."

J.W. squeezed my hand.

The week leading to Spring Fling flew by, bringing perfect weather at last. Spring is by far my favorite season. Everything seemed to be starting over, including me. My back looked the same, but my face had cleared, just as Dr.

T said. If only the new antibiotic I was taking would kick in fast, and keep it that way.

Friday afternoon, the day of Spring Fling, we had early dismissal and I went for a long walk, coming home energized. Jenna, Wendy, and I had originally planned to all get ready together, but decided it would be easier to do it on our own, so we'd have time to meet the guys for dinner. I set out my dress: a bronze-taffeta sheath, simple yet elegant. It had a low neckline but a high back, which was just what I needed. And it was practically brand-new—I'd worn it only once, to Danny's bar mitzvah. I combed my closet for my brown, rhinestone strappy heels as Megan, sitting on my bed watching, rifled through my jewelry box. Twirling a strand of fake pearls on her arm, she asked, "Are you going to make out with J.W. tonight?"

I wasn't prepared for that one! Megan's not even into boys. "Do you think I'd tell you?"

"I'd tell *you*."

"It better not be any time soon!" I laughed.

She tried a different tactic. "Have you and J.W. kissed at *all*?"

She looked so eager, her heart-shaped face fixed on me, that I tossed her a bone. "Maybe."

"That means yes," she said. "Does Mom know?"

"I don't think so." It was unusual, now that I thought about it, because I have always told Mom everything. But between her hectic work schedule and my skin problems and the Wacky Water mess, Mom and I hadn't discussed J.W.—or anything else—lately.

"Do you think Mom will ever fall in love again?" Megan asked.

"I have no idea." I peeled off my workout clothes, tossed them in the hamper, and marched into the bathroom. "She's not in any hurry."

Megan stood outside the door. "Do you think Dad and Kim are in love?"

"Well, *yeah* . . . they live together."

"Kim would make a good stepmom," she said solemnly.

I didn't want to get into it, so I shut the door, blasted the shower, and stepped in. I still had the image in my head of Dad and Kim at Mariano's, their hands intertwined like lovesick teenagers, even though Dad's forty-two! And in less than twenty-four hours, I'd get to see the lovebirds again, since Megan and I were heading to Albuquerque . . . for the entire spring break.

At 6:30 p.m., I was ready to go. I'd painted my nails a dusty bronze, blow-dried my hair, and set it with Velcro rollers—the way stylists usually do—creating long, cascading curls. Then I expertly applied base, shimmery powder, and concealer to even out my complexion. Last, I swiped on sparkly copper eye shadow, dark-brown eyeliner, black mascara, apricot lip gloss, and two squirts of Mom's jasmine blossom perfume.

I rushed downstairs, where Aunt Barb and Megan were waiting, armed with cameras. Aunt Barb tossed me her rust cashmere shawl, to complete the look.

"A bronzed goddess!" she declared, taking a picture.

Thanks to my fake tan. The bronzed look was growing on me.

"Puh-*leeze*!" But I felt pretty darn good. Tonight, I could relax. "Where's Mom?"

"Well," Barb said, "there's been a slight hitch. Linda got stuck at work with some difficult couple. She feels terrible that she can't make it home in time."

"Mom's not here?" Work was more important than seeing me before the most important dance of my life, so far? Never mind that she was supposed to drive Jenna, Wendy, and me to Nina's, the French bistro we were going to for dinner. "Who's going to take us?"

Aunt Barb clicked her black Converse sneakers together. "Chauffeur Barb at your service."

"I call shotgun!" Megan chimed in.

The three of us hustled into the car and zoomed across town to fetch the girls. Jenna looked beautiful in a little black dress, and Wendy, no surprise, was a knockout in a strapless fuchsia gown.

"You guys look incredible!" I sang.

"We *all* do," Jenna said. "Our dates should approve."

"This isn't a *date*," Wendy reminded her. "It's a group outing."

Jenna clucked her tongue. "My bad."

It was like Wendy and Jenna had switched places. Who could have imagined?

At Nina's, J.W., Matt, and Theo were already seated at a corner table in identical white shirts, dark suits, and ties. I'd never seen J.W. in a suit and it meant a lot to me that he'd dressed up because, even though we were *supposed* to for the dance, I knew plenty of guys wouldn't. He rose from the table and pulled out my chair, smiling at me.

Seconds later, a college-aged waitress appeared to take our order. We all got pasta dishes, but J.W. finished by saying, "And we'd like to see the wine list, miss."

Matt coughed, Theo rolled his eyes, Jenna shook her head, and Wendy covered her mouth with a napkin.

The waitress smirked. "Certainly, sir. I'll just need to see your I.D."

Jenna nudged me, and I nudged her back. What did she expect me to do? J.W. reached for his wallet, whipped out a driver's license, and handed it over.

The waitress inspected it. "Your older brother?"

"I don't have an older brother," J.W. replied smoothly. It was a lie—his brother was a junior at U.C. Santa Barbara. "So how 'bout that wine list?"

The waitress dropped the fake license on the table. "How 'bout we forget this happened, so I don't have to report you to the manager?"

J.W. flashed an uneasy smile. "We'd just like—"

"Water," Theo spoke up.

"Me, too," Matt said.

"Fine," J.W. gave in.

"I'll have a Sprite," Wendy said.

"Make that two," Jenna added.

"Three," I said. I'd cut way back on sugary cola, but I was craving fizzy carbonation like crazy.

"Water and Sprite it is." The waitress dashed off.

"That girl has a major attitude," J.W. said.

"*She* has attitude?" Theo snorted.

Matt, sitting *thisclose* to Jenna, asked J.W., "Are you trying to get us arrested? That would really make the night memorable."

"You can't blame a guy for trying," said Wendy.

"That's what I'm talkin' about!" J.W. said. They clinked imaginary glasses.

I didn't know what to make of it. Plenty of kids my age drink, but I don't, and I wished J.W. hadn't tried to order it here.

He whispered into my ear, "I swear I'm not a boozer. I just want tonight to be special."

At least we were on the same page about that.

Jeremy, J.W.'s brother, was home for spring break, so he picked us up after dinner. The six of us managed to squeeze into the car. "Bro," he said to J.W. first thing, "have you seen my driver's license?"

Matt and Theo hooted with laughter as J.W. handed it over.

"I *thought* so," Jeremy muttered.

Jenna nudged me again.

At school, the cafeteria had been converted into a futuristic club, with silver balloons and strobe lights everywhere. It was packed. We made the rounds saying hi to everyone, but I was focused on J.W. standing beside me, his hand on my back. The last few weeks were starting to feel like nothing more than a bad dream. Wendy and I howled when Jenna and Matt hit the dance floor and Jenna let loose, shaking it like I'd never seen. A DJ with a mohawk stood on a makeshift stage, hollering, *"Let's get this party started!"* while everyone cheered.

Wendy demonstrated her moves in front of Theo. "Wanna dance?" she asked, when he didn't take the hint.

"Maybe later." Theo winced, as if he was in pain. He didn't have his cane.

Wendy started dancing alone. She'll dance anywhere, anytime. Not me. Thankfully, I've never been asked to dance for an audition—I'm not sure I could pull it off. Wendy's got rhythm, and the way she sways her hips guarantees male attention. Both Theo and J.W. watched her as I watched them, so I didn't notice Wendy raise her arms over her head, tilting the plastic cup of punch she clutched in her hand . . . until she splashed cold, red liquid down the front of my dress.

"AAAAGH!" I screeched.

Wendy clapped her hand over her mouth. "Omigosh, I'm so sorry, Olivia! It was an ACCIDENT!"

Worse: J.W. was laughing!

Wendy gave in, too, the pair of them busting up.

"It's not funny, guys! Not funny AT ALL!" I shouted.

J.W. reached for me, but I shook him off. "It's sorta funny," he said.

Wendy tried to keep a straight face. "I'll buy you a new dress, I swear."

Given Wendy's generous allowance, she could buy me an entire spring wardrobe, no sweat. But that wouldn't help me right now.

"*Thanks,*" I snapped. I didn't want to act bratty, but I was mad. And a total mess. I turned and zigzagged through a sea of writhing bodies to the refreshment table, grabbing a stack of napkins. Dabbing at my dress, I glanced back to see if either Wendy or J.W. was following me. They weren't. They were, in fact, on the dance floor, joining a conga line! This wasn't turning out like the romantic night I'd envisioned, and it was all Wendy's fault.

Theo caught up to me. "Need some help?"

Then he leaned against the table. Touching Theo's arm, I asked, "Wanna go sit down?" I wanted to escape and I had a feeling Theo did, too.

We walked out to the courtyard, where a few couples mingled. The night air was balmy, but peaceful. We sat down on a stone bench and Theo squirmed out of his coat jacket, draping it across my damp dress.

"Thanks."

"No prob." Gazing upward, he noted, "It's a full moon."

I wasn't in the mood for stargazing, but the silver moon was breathtaking, hanging so low in the sky it looked like we could reach out and grab it.

"Are you into astronomy?" I asked.

"Yeah," he said shyly. "We have a telescope at home, and camp out a lot. You can see a million stars in the desert, even shooting ones. Well, meteors really."

"You camp?" Right as I said it, I wanted to kick myself.

"Sure." He paused. "J.W. told you I have juvenile arthritis, huh? But it's not that bad. It just slows me down a little."

I glanced at Theo. He didn't look weak or sickly. He was actually pretty muscular. And he seemed so sure of himself. "J.W. said you've had it for a long time."

"Five years," Theo answered, still looking at the sky. "It's pretty well controlled, but it flares up sometimes. When I was younger, kids used to make fun of me for using the cane. But people I'm around a lot don't even notice it now. I just didn't want to bring it to a dance."

"Why do you use the cane, exactly?" I hoped Theo didn't mind my asking.

"My hands and feet get stiff and swollen sometimes, and the cane helps. I'm lucky the pain's more in my left foot. If it was bad in both, I might have to use a walker." He paused. "Can I ask *you* a question?"

"Sure."

"Why were you at Dr. T's office?"

I didn't hesitate. "I have acne. Nodular acne, which Dr. T says is tougher to treat, though it comes and goes."

"Have you told J.W.?"

I sucked in my breath. "No. He thinks I have allergic reactions."

"I won't tell him," Theo promised. I hadn't known Theo long, but I trusted him. "And don't be too mad at J.W. about the punch thing. His sense of humor's kind of . . ."

"Juvenile?"

"Yeah." Theo grinned. "Juvenile."

"He and Wendy have that in common."

"I noticed," Theo said. "But she acts stuck-up."

That took me by surprise. "You think?"

"Definitely," he answered, and then backpedaled. "No offense. I'm sure she's a good friend. I'm just not a big fan."

So he hadn't wanted to be set up with her. "Right now, that makes two of us."

We went back inside a few minutes later. Theo insisted I could wear his jacket. J.W. came up to us, with Danny and Ed close behind. J.W. was slightly sweaty from dancing. He inhaled helium from a silver balloon and squeaked, *"Where'd you guys go?"* All the guys laughed, and I did, too.

"We were stargazing," I said.

J.W. held out a hand. "How 'bout dancing?" To Theo, he said, "Wendy's getting more punch."

"Thanks for the warning," Theo said dryly.

J.W.'s arms encircled my waist. Guiding me to the dance floor, he asked, "What's with the jacket?"

"Theo let me borrow it," I said. "To cover the punch stain, remember?"

"Was your dress expensive?" J.W. asked.

"It doesn't matter." Mom had bought it marked down, but it was ruined now. "Anyway, it's Wendy I'm mad at." *She should've followed me when I walked off,* I thought. *She should've tried to help.* But then, so should've J.W.

"She feels really bad about it," J.W. insisted. "Don't be mad."

I didn't want to dwell on it. "I'll get over it."

He nestled his head close to mine. "I can't believe you'll be gone the whole break, Olivia. I wish you were staying here."

I'd have given anything to spend it with J.W. instead of Dad. "Me, too."

"I'll text you every day," J.W. vowed.

Then he held me tight, and we swayed together.

Chapter Fourteen

SPRING BREAK

While Megan and I finished packing Saturday morning, Mom ran back and forth into our rooms giving last-minute instructions. "If you need *anything* while you're gone, girls, call me." To Mom, being in Albuquerque is like being stranded in the wilderness.

"We know, Mom," I replied, stuffing a handful of underwear in my suitcase.

"Did you double-check that you packed your anti-biotics and prescription cleansers?" she asked.

"*Yessss.*" Mom had apologized five times for not seeing me before the dance, but I was still a bit miffed. It wasn't worth getting into, though, since we had a plane to catch and Mom was in panic mode.

"Megan?" she cried. "Do you have the emergency

contact info list I gave you? Don't lose it!"

Mom was worked up for one particular reason, I knew: Dad would be busy at work all week, as usual, leaving Kim in charge.

As we drove to the airport, I considered the pros and cons of the trip:

PROS
1) J.W. would miss me.
2) I could sleep in every morning.
3) Dad would buy us stuff.

CONS
1) What would Dad and I talk about?
2) What would Kim and I do?
3) What would J.W. do without me
   around?

After Mom parked, checked our baggage, and walked us to the security checkpoint, she smothered Megan and me in her arms, saying, "I'm really going to miss you two!"

I felt bad for Mom. Spring break, for us, meant goofing off. But goofing off doesn't fit into Mom's schedule. While Megan and I were relaxing and eating out and shopping, Mom would be working and then coming home to an empty house. Even Barb wouldn't be there because her culinary academy also had spring break—she was headed to Cancún with some friends.

Mom goes to PTA meetings, parent nights, and bake sales, but she doesn't hang out with friends anymore. She says she doesn't have the time.

"We'll only be gone a week," I reminded her. "It will fly by."

"I know, I know." Mom blew her nose. "Be good, and be careful! And if you need anything—"

"We'll call," Megan and I finished.

Mom stood there waving as Megan and I went through the security line and metal detector. We turned and waved back before walking to the gate. In her white tee and khaki capri pants, Mom looked cute . . . and oblivious to three middle-aged businessmen eyeing her.

On the plane, Megan immediately popped her iPod earbuds in. She can't get enough of Taylor Swift-wannabes. I'm more into Lady Gaga myself, but I wanted to sleep. I'd gotten only five hours last night because I kept replaying J.W.'s steamy good-night kiss, which he planted on me right before the cafeteria lights came on. I'd felt amazing then, but exhausted now. I wedged my head in the window crook, trying to get comfortable.

When the plane took off, I closed my eyes and my mind drifted to a trip that Mom, Dad, Megan, and I took to New York City a year-and-a-half ago. We stayed at the Plaza Hotel and hit the hot spots—the Natural History Museum, Broadway, Rockefeller Center, and Central Park. We went in early December, and the city was one gigantic holiday display. It was the first and only time I've been there, and our best family vacation by far. Flying home, we each named our favorite part of the trip. For Dad, it was taking Megan and me to the FAO Schwarz toy store and seeing our faces light up. Making us happy made *him* feel happy, he'd said. Little did I know our days as a family unit were dwindling. As soon as we returned home, Dad disappeared into work, and Mom became quiet. He moved out New Year's Day.

"Olivia, wake up!" Megan shook me. "We're here!"

My eyes shot open, jolting me back to the present as we landed in Albuquerque.

Kim was waiting for us in the baggage claim. She looked stylishly casual in a black tank top, gray spandex pants, oversized sunglasses, and flip-flops. Waving enthusiastically, she called, "Hi, girls!"

Megan scanned the crowd. "Where's Dad?"

I *knew* what came next.

Kim picked up Megan's duffel bag. "He's . . . at work."

Megan's body drooped. "It's *Saturday*!"

"He wanted to be here, but he's prepping for an important case," Kim said cheerfully—too cheerfully—as she led us to her blue Prius in the parking garage. "There's a hip downtown café we can go to for lunch. You girls will love it!"

The midday sun beat down on us during the twenty-minute drive. We pulled up to the Cosmic Café, a coral-pink shack jammed with college students.

"I'm a little old for this joint," Kim said. "But I love the vibe."

Suddenly I wondered if Dad's long work hours made Kim lonely, the way Mom used to be. She probably came here just to be around people, even if they *were* younger.

After we were seated in a vinyl booth and ordered soup-and-sandwich combos, Kim removed her sunglasses and asked, "How are things, girls?" Kim is vague like that. She doesn't ask specific questions about friends or family or school, so it's hard to tell what she wants to hear.

But Megan plunged right in. "We're studying global warming in science class."

"That's great!" Kim said. "Kids need to realize the horrible damage being inflicted on our planet."

"Um-hmm." Megan was right there with her. "I'm secretary of the environmental club."

"Excellent!" Kim glanced out the window.

"Waiting for Dad?" I asked. I'd seen Mom do it a million times.

Kim squeezed lemon into her iced tea. "I left him a message when I got to the airport. I was hoping he'd join us. He's really been looking forward to spending time with you two."

"Dad works a ton," I stated matter-of-factly, in case Kim was in denial. But I didn't use the W-word— workaholic—because I wasn't sure how she would react.

"Yes, I'm aware," Kim said calmly. "Work-life balance

is a big issue, in my book. One that your dad and I are working out together."

Her directness took me by surprise. Score one for Kim.

Megan twirled the straw in her fizzy orange soda. "Mom and Dad didn't work things out. They got divorced."

"Yes." Kim cupped her glass in her hands. "Your dad has serious regrets about that. Sometimes couples don't make it, no matter how much they try. But he loves you girls, and he doesn't want to repeat the same mistakes."

Then why was Dad at work and not here?

Our food arrived, and we all dug in. Kim didn't bring Dad up again and neither did I. His mistakes were clear to me, but Kim would have to find out for herself.

Back at their one-story, eco-friendly adobe house, Megan and I played cards and read in the backyard while Kim gardened. I like the idea of gardening, but I hate getting dirt under my fingernails. I was impressed that Kim grew her own vegetables, so she and Dad had fresh organic food to eat all the time.

As the sun set, I crawled into the hammock while Megan turned cartwheels on the grass. She's in constant motion from morning until bedtime—when her head finally hits the pillow, she passes out. Hearing the wind chimes on the patio, I closed my eyes . . . and dozed off. This time, it was Dad who woke me up, calling, "Hey, sleepyhead."

I sat up startled, forgetting where I was for a moment.

Dad steadied the hammock so I didn't roll off. Gruffly, he patted my shoulder and said, "Glad you're here, hon. Dinner's ready." He leaned down and kissed my forehead.

We ate outside at the patio table. Kim had prepared a simple vegan meal: arugula salad, whole-wheat penne, and spinach balls that tasted surprisingly good.

"Garlic is the magic ingredient," she informed Megan and me. "Herbs, onions, and sea salt are also terrific flavor enhancers."

"Aunt Barb uses them," Megan said. "She's the best cook, but she's not a vegan."

Over lunch, Kim had talked about how meat production leaves a huge carbon imprint, and how most animals are treated inhumanely before being slaughtered. The process sounded disgusting, and I was determined to cut down on meat and dairy. Besides sparing innocent animals, it also might help my skin. Megan vowed to go vegan, but the second she laid eyes on a cheeseburger, I knew she'd cave.

"What about your mom?" Kim asked. "Is she a good cook?"

"She's good at ordering takeout," said Megan.

Kim and Dad laughed. I didn't join in. Mom may not be a gourmet chef, but she has plenty of other interests: knitting and solving crossword puzzles, for example. She used to hike and ride her bike, too, before she started working.

"So," Dad said to me. "What's new at school?"

"I was nominated to be a freshman Ambassador next year." I knew that would thrill him.

"Excellent!" He nodded his approval. "What do Ambassadors do?"

"Schmooze with guests at special school events . . . show them around."

Megan jumped in. "And hang out with her Ambassador boyfriend, J.W. That's why she wants to do it."

I couldn't deny it—being with J.W. was the best part.

"A boyfriend, hmm?" Kim winked at me.

Dad coughed into his napkin. We don't discuss my love life. "Well, congratulations. I'm really proud of you, Olivia. What's happening with Wicked Water?"

I couldn't tell if he was joking. "It's *Wacky* Water."

"Right, right. Wacky Water."

I carefully considered my answer. Given Dad's general objections, a full report didn't seem wise. "We shoot the second commercial soon."

"Is Eleanor treating you alright?" Dad's not a big Eleanor fan. *That* I understood.

"Um, yeah." I focused on my salad. "She thinks Wacky Water could be a major breakthrough—"

"—if Olivia's face clears up," Megan finished.

Bigmouth.

Kim refilled my water glass. "Olivia looks lovely."

"You should have seen her two weeks ago," Megan said. "Her face was like a pepperoni pizza!"

"*Thanks.*" I glared at her. I turned back to Dad and Kim and said, "The medicine I took wasn't working. My skin's okay now because I had cortisone shots."

Dad nearly spit out his water. "You had *what*?"

"The dermatologist recommended it. But they don't last long, so she prescribed another antibiotic."

He shook his head in disbelief. "And neither you nor your mother bothered to discuss it with me?"

I resisted pointing out that Mom has primary custody. Legally, Dad doesn't have a say. Also, I'd begged Mom to keep it just between us. "It's one measly prescription. It's not like I'm taking heavy drugs."

"I hate that you're on medication because of some pushy agent."

Here we go.

"Using antibiotics for an extended amount of time isn't healthy," Dad continued, like he was a medical expert. "Your body builds up immunity, and that makes future antibiotics less effective. Any doctor will tell you that. Prescription drugs are overkill for a minor condition."

Minor condition? I dropped my fork, and it clattered against the wrought-iron table. "Sometimes my skin breaks out bad, Dad. You're just not around to see it."

He ignored the dig. "Acne is unpleasant, but not permanent. It may just be something you have to live with, for a while."

"I *have* been living with it. The last Wacky

Water shoot was a disaster!"

There—I'd said it.

He threw his hands up. "It always comes back to these commercials."

"No, it's not just that. It's school, too . . . the way people see and talk to me sometimes." My voice caught.

"What about natural remedies?" Kim suggested. "There's tea tree oil, zinc, black currant seed oil, aloe vera . . ."

"I need something with more of a guarantee," I said. "My acting career depends on it."

"Does acting mean *that* much?" Dad asked.

I looked him in the eye. "Yes. And if this medicine doesn't work, I'll just take something stronger."

"If it comes to that," he said in a stern voice, "there will be more discussion. For now, let's just agree to disagree."

Dad is such a lawyer.

Chapter Fifteen

ALL IN THE FAMILY

Dad worked all week but came home early each night—earlier than he used to with us, anyway. Kim took a week off from the exercise studio where she taught, and showed Megan and me around town. Most days, we went out for lunch, saw a movie, and hiked in the hills near their home. Kim was actually easy to be around—friendly and talkative, but not *too* chummy, which I appreciated. And she introduced Megan and me to new things: shopping at the local farmer's market and trying a few yoga classes. They were challenging, but doable, and I felt great afterward. At night, after dinner, Dad, Kim, Megan, and I played board games. Dad even muted ESPN and CNBC—the two channels he's addicted to—watching them closed-captioned. I could tell he was trying.

Thursday night, Dad came home extra early to take us to an IMAX theater. We watched a 3-D documentary on the Grand Canyon and I felt like I was there in a helicopter, soaring over cliffs and swooping into the canyons. It was amazing, but I got slightly nauseous.

"We really wanted to see this film with you guys," Dad said as we left the theater.

Megan took the bait. "Why, Daddy?"

"Kim and I are camping in the Grand Canyon this July. And we want to bring you girls."

"Camping? I thought you preferred four-star hotels," I said.

"For business trips. For adventure, nothing beats being in the great outdoors."

Someone had kidnapped my father and replaced him with a nature lover. Dad has never opted to rough it, vacationwise. We've always stayed in luxury hotels—not mesh tents. Kim's earthy approach to life was certainly rubbing off on him.

"What about bears?" Megan asked. She's terrified of them, even though she's never run into one.

Dad tousled her hair. "Not where we'll be."

"Then I'm in!" she said, skipping toward the car.

"My birthday's in July," I reminded him. I didn't have a set plan, but I wasn't sure I wanted to spend it camping with Dad.

"So is mine!" Kim said. "When's yours?"

"July eleventh."

"I'm July seventeenth. That makes us both Cancers."

"Huh?" Megan asked.

I bumped her hip with mine. "That's our astrological sign, dummy."

"What's my sign, again?"

"You're a Pisces, the peaceful fish."

"That sounds way better than a Cancer."

"Well, we can *all* celebrate," Dad said. "Doesn't trekking through the Grand Canyon sound like a memorable life experience, Olivia?"

"We better check with Mom." Theo had sparked my interest in camping, the night of Spring Fling, but I wasn't sold yet.

Saturday morning I woke up to the mouthwatering aroma of fresh-roasted coffee. I detest the *taste* of coffee, but I love the smell. After breakfast, the four of us were driving to Santa Fe for the day. I'd been having slight cramps since yesterday, so I checked things out in the bathroom. Sure enough, I had my second period. This time I was prepared! I'd packed minipads and tampons in my luggage, just in case, and stowed them under the guest bathroom sink. I reached for a pad, wishing Mom was there.

Next I stared into the mirror. As Dr. T had predicted, my acne was making a comeback. Several pimples were slowly forming on my face, in various stages. And, unlike the previous zits, these new ones were hard, blistery— cystic. The worst kind, Dr. T had said.

"Olivia?" Dad knocked on the door. "Do you want some breakfast?"

What I wanted was for Dad to see exactly what I was dealing with. I swung open the bathroom door. Dad had a coffee mug in one hand and *The Wall Street Journal* in the other. Seeing me, his mouth formed a giant circle.

"*This,*" I announced, "is why I need medication."

After we had all piled into Dad's sedan, I leaned against the car window, watching brown hills speed by on the interstate. I preferred Northern California greenery, even if the freeways there were clogged. But no scenery could have lifted my spirits today.

"You girls okay back there?" Dad asked.

"Yep," Megan said. I didn't respond.

"Alright, then," Dad said. He clicked on the satellite radio, tuning in to a baseball game.

Five minutes later, my cell phone rang. "Jenna!"

"Hey, O. How are ya?"

I automatically felt better hearing her voice. "Okay. How 'bout you?"

"So-so. Matt's in Santa Cruz, and my granddad's visiting all week. If I have to play one more round of gin rummy, I may scream. How are you holding up?"

Jenna knows Dad and I have issues, so she got it when I said, "As expected. Have you seen anyone? What's Wendy up to?"

"I'm, uh, not sure. . . . I haven't really seen her." Jenna doesn't stumble over words unless she's saying something that makes her uncomfortable. But I couldn't concentrate because Dad had cranked up the radio to hear the Yankees-Angels game, two teams he *doesn't even like.*

Raising my voice, I asked, "What do you mean?" But there was no answer—only static. "Jenna, are you there?"

"Olivia!" Dad yelled. "I'm trying to listen to the game. You can talk to your girlfriend later."

"You hate the Yankees!"

"I like baseball," Dad replied. "And when you're old enough to drive, Olivia, you can decide what to listen to in *your* car. In the meantime, no phone calls unless it's your mother."

I dropped the phone in my purse. This was Dad at his worst—controlling and sports-obsessed.

He shot me a steely glance in the rearview mirror. "Let's try to have a nice day."

I pulled out my iPod so I wouldn't have to listen to Dad or his loud, stupid baseball.

Kim patted his shoulder soothingly.

"Why are you being such a jerk?" Megan whispered to me. "It's not our fault you have acne."

I hated them all.

• • •

Downtown Santa Fe was a bustling, colorful mix of tourists and restaurants and shops. It was my second time in the city and I really liked it, but I couldn't enjoy it. I had the nagging sense that Jenna had kept something from me, something about Wendy. Or was I imagining it? Nothing had changed between Wendy and me, exactly. I just hadn't felt ultraclose to her since our parents separated and we spent hours swapping sad stories. It was the only time I told Wendy more than Jenna because we both understood, and talking about it helped. But the more time that passed, the less Wendy and I shared.

Sure, the Spring Fling punch-spill had been an accident, but instead of acting sorry, Wendy had danced with my *date*. What kind of friend did that? J.W. had seemed more worried that I was mad. And now he was being supersweet, texting me daily, telling me to hurry up and come home.

I skipped the last art gallery that the others ducked into and waited on a bench outside. I pulled my cell out of my purse and tried calling Jenna back, but it went straight to voicemail.

Two teenage guys walked by. One with a buzz cut sneered at me and said, "Who's calling *you*?" The other one laughed.

Once they were gone, I whipped out my compact mirror, hands shaking, and swallowed back tears. My morning makeup was long gone, revealing eight gruesome pimples. I had never felt so . . . *ugly*. It was obvious why cystic acne sucked the most. They were small, but fierce-looking boils that no one could hide. *What if medication didn't work? What if I had acne for years?* I sat there in a daze until Megan, Kim, and Dad came out and saw me dabbing my eyes.

"Can I do anything, Olivia?" Dad asked.

"No."

Didn't he get it by now?

In a nearby park, Kim spread out a quilt and set out peanut butter and jelly sandwiches, fruit salad, veggie kebobs, and juice. I picked at my food.

"We should head home," Dad said uneasily, after they polished off the rest.

"Can we stay a little longer?" Megan stared longingly at the playground, giving him her best puppy-dog expression. It doesn't work with Mom, but it never misses with Dad.

"Sure, hon," he said.

I jumped up. "I'm going for a walk."

Dad scrambled to his feet. "I'll come with you."

A leisurely stroll with Dad was the last thing I wanted. We entered a wooded trail and I speed-walked, trying to get ahead, but he fell in step with me.

"I'm sorry if I upset you earlier," he said. "No matter what you believe, Olivia, I hate seeing you so unhappy."

I stumbled on some rocks, and fell down. Then I did something I never thought I'd do—I burst into tears, right in front of Dad. In an instant, he was holding me, lifting me up. Stroking my hair, he said, "I understand why you're so sad, honey."

How could he?

"I had acne when I was a teenager, too," he said.

"You did?" I stepped back.

"I had it really bad for a few years. I didn't go on one date my freshman or sophomore year of high school."

"So, what happened?"

"My skin cleared up, eventually."

"Why didn't you tell me before?"

He brushed dirt off his jeans. "Honestly, I hoped I wouldn't need to. I've read that acne is hereditary, but my parents didn't have it, and I figured you and Megan wouldn't, either. When I first noticed, at Mariano's, I thought your case was milder than mine. I hate that you inherited this from me, Olivia. When I had acne, there wasn't much to do but wait it out."

"Then why don't you want me taking medicine?"

Dad hesitated. "I don't want you to take it if it isn't necessary. And I do think the stress of being in commercials is a contributing factor."

"I *like* being in commercials!" I stated, for the millionth time.

"Still," Dad said, "it's not the healthiest environment for a young girl."

"I'm not that young, Dad. . . . I'm almost fourteen."

"I can see you're growing up. And until today, I didn't fully realize—"

"That I'm hideous?"

"Olivia." He grimaced. "Try to be reasonable."

Being reasonable is Dad's answer to *everything*.

"Having acne sucks, Dad. I'm screwing up in a national campaign, and my boyfriend thinks I have allergies because I'm too embarrassed to tell him the truth. What if I end up losing both?"

"If you do," he said calmly, "then neither is worth having. You have a family who loves you, Olivia, and that's the most important thing in life. You'll get through this, and I'll do whatever I can to help."

"You *left*, Dad," I said, the words bitter in my throat. "You moved here, and you have a new girlfriend and a new life. So just forget it!"

I backtracked through the woods toward the park, moving fast.

"Olivia!" He was right behind me. "I understand you're upset, but please give me a chance. I'm truly sorry."

Dad was finally sorry and I didn't even care. What was he apologizing for, anyway? Giving me acne? Leaving us? Or for just being so hard to talk to? Trying to pin him down was useless. No matter how sorry Dad was, I knew he didn't have any easy answers.

Chapter Sixteen

HOMECOMING

The flight home Sunday was delayed for three *lo-o-ong* hours on the runway due to a mechanical malfunction, so Megan and I didn't land in San Francisco until ten p.m. Mom was waiting for us at the airport, yawning and glassy-eyed.

"Mom!" Megan raced over to her.

"Hi, girls!" Mom scooped both of us into her arms. Then, looking down at my crusted, spotty face, she said, "Oh, sweetie."

My eyes welled with tears, not just from Mom's comment, but from the whole bad weekend. The only conversation Dad and I had after arguing in the woods yesterday was awkward small talk on the way to the airport. I didn't blame him about the acne—or even for being concerned about the medication, so much—but it was just another issue dividing us.

"I-I don't feel well," I said. "I better stay home tomorrow."

"Olivia . . . are you really sick?" Mom asked.

"Sick of Dad," Megan jumped in. "They had a huge fight." I hadn't told Megan, but she'd figured it out.

Mom kissed my pimply forehead. "Let's see how you feel tomorrow. And I'll call Dr. T first thing."

Megan tugged on Mom's sleeve. "Am I going to get acne when I'm older?"

"I don't know, hon," Mom said honestly. "Hopefully not."

Megan just shrugged. "Well, *I'm* going to school tomorrow. I haven't seen my friends for nine whole days!"

At 7:00 a.m. Monday, I shivered in bed, doing my best to convince Mom that I was truly ill.

"If you're not better by this afternoon, I'm taking you to the doctor," Mom warned, as she headed out the door with Megan. "And I'm coming home to check on you at lunch."

So she wasn't totally buying it. I felt a stab of guilt, but not enough to go to school and see people—especially J.W.

I spent the morning lying on the den sofa, feeling tired

and sad. Outside the bay windows, thunder rumbled and lightning crackled in a late April storm. I huddled deeper on the couch and turned on the TV.

That's when I saw Me. Or, I should say, the Old Me, in the Zit Zapper commercial I'd shot months ago. In the twenty-second clip, I skipped through a flowery garden—my peaches-and-cream complexion shining in the sun.

I clicked off the remote and lay there in the shadows. Despite being in commercials, I've never considered myself a vain person. I don't have expensive haircuts and trendy makeup and designer clothes, like some of my friends. I don't even love shopping! Yet now I was consumed with my appearance 24/7. In one month, my face had dramatically changed. A pimple or two, I could handle—everyone gets them sometimes. But mine weren't ordinary, run-of-the-mill zits. These scaly, cystic lumps seemed to have a life of their own.

Then I thought of Theo. He was living with a serious, debilitating disease that might easily cause permanent damage. While visiting Dad and Kim, I'd researched juvenile rheumatoid arthritis online. JRA could go into remission as people got older . . . but it could also get worse. Theo might grow up to be a normal, healthy adult—or he could have crooked, deformed joints. And he had no idea which way it would go.

Me, on the other hand? I could be scarred for life, literally, but it was my pride that hurt more than anything.

That and feeling like how I looked was out of my control. From week to week—even day to day—I might look good or bad. I couldn't count on medicine solving this for me.

At lunchtime, Mom came home with a takeout order of steaming chicken noodle soup. Pure comfort food. She brought it to me, along with a glass of milk and saltine crackers, on a tray. Gently setting it down, she asked, "How do you feel?"

"So-so."

Mom kicked off her heels and sat down at the other end of the sofa. "I called Dr. T's office. She said we should give the Minocycline a little more time."

I forced a soggy cracker down my throat. "Maybe we should have tried a stronger drug. Maybe then I wouldn't look like a freak."

"Who knows how fast it would have worked? Or the side effects?" Mom sighed. "I wish you didn't have to take anything. I wish I had a magic wand to banish your acne for good."

"That would be nice." I attempted a smile. Feeling sorry for myself wasn't fun.

Mom returned it. "Let's talk about something else. What happened between you and your dad?"

Ugh—from one bad subject to another.

"It might help you to get it out," she said.

So I did. I described the entire week to Mom, beginning with Dad not picking us up at the airport, to arguing with him in the Santa Fe woods.

"I never knew James had acne!" she said.

"Dad isn't big on sharing," I pointed out.

"Your dad isn't the best at communicating, it's true, but that's because he's a shy and reserved person. His heart's in the right place. He loves you and Megan very much."

"Then why did he move?"

"I wasn't thrilled, either, but work has always been his escape." Mom was quiet a moment. "There's something I haven't told you before, Olivia. I'd rather Megan not know yet, but I think you should. Your dad and I deciding to divorce wasn't exactly mutual. Marital counseling hadn't helped, and I knew your father wasn't going to change. So I asked him for a divorce."

Somehow, Mom's words didn't surprise me. Deep inside I'd known she was the unhappy one all along. "Dad didn't want a divorce?" I asked.

"Not at first." She shook her head. "But he came to accept it, and we're both happier now. I don't want *you* to be unhappy, Olivia, blaming your dad for something he didn't do. Think about what he does do—calling and seeing you and Megan often. He's not perfect—who is?— but he tries. You both could try a little harder."

Tuesday morning, I dragged myself to school. Even with foundation, concealer, and powder, I was an ugly sight. Head down, I cruised through the crowded halls until I reached Jenna's locker. We'd traded messages, but hadn't spoken. If anyone could cheer me up, it was Jenna.

Unfortunately, when she saw me, she gasped.

"That bad, hmm?" My hopes sank low...low...lower.

"Is this why you stayed home yesterday?" she asked.

"Yep," I replied, my mouth trembling.

Jenna squeezed my arm. "Why don't you come over after school?"

"If I make it through the day here."

"Are you leaving?"

"No," I said. Mom wouldn't allow it. "I'll just hide out in the bathroom . . . or library . . . or nurse's office."

"Until your face clears up?" Jenna asked. "That's not exactly realistic, O."

The way Jenna said it reminded me of Dad. "Don't start in on me, too," I said.

"I'm not! But you can't just avoid people. I know you're depressed about this, O, but you've gotta deal."

What did Jenna know about dealing with acne? Or feeling depressed about anything? She was smarter and more together than any adult I knew. "I could out myself in the morning announcements," I said sarcastically. *"I'm Olivia Hughes, and I have cystic acne."*

She pursed her lips. "At least you'd finally be telling the truth."

Jenna's remark stung, but before I could respond, I saw Wendy, J.W., Danny, and Ed down the hall, coming our way.

"Hi, guys!" Wendy waved to us.

If only I could disappear.

"Olivia!" J.W. called out. Then, getting closer, his smile

evaporated. We stood inches apart, neither of us speaking.

"*Now* do you see?" Danny said, elbowing J.W.

Danny and I had walked into school at the same time. When he saw me and gawked, I'd run ahead. I was cornered now. No more hiding or faking or lying or hoping that J.W. might come down with another contagious illness.

This was it. . . .

"Olivia." J.W.'s voice was low. "What happened?"

Wendy beat me to it. "Acne. I *knew* it!"

Why did she have to sound so gleeful? What was wrong with my friends? They were supposed to help me out, not drag me down. I could do that all by myself.

"It's on her back, too," Ed informed everyone. "I saw it sitting behind her in math. You should stick to turtlenecks, Olivia."

"You're such a jerk!" I yelled.

"Better than being a Zitface."

"Shut up, Ed," J.W. broke in. But he was already backing away from me. "I'm really, really sorry, Olivia. . . ."

Everyone was sorry. Well, I was tired of hearing it. I didn't need their pity—I needed someone who understood. I could tell it wasn't going to be J.W.

"I'm sorry, too," I said numbly. Maybe I was wrong to keep him in the dark as long as I did.

"I'll, um." J.W. paused. "I'll see you later, okay?"

"Okay," I said, but he was too far away to hear.

Chapter Seventeen

CANNED

The next two weeks were a depressing blur. I saw J.W. every day at school, and every time he smiled, waved . . . and kept on going. Without a word, I'd been demoted from girlfriend to barely a friend. My heart ached whenever I saw him. And every day when I got home, I hoped that J.W. would call, e-mail, or even just text, saying *something*. But he didn't do any of those things. His silence was loud and clear.

Jenna said he wasn't worth my time, while Wendy kept asking if I hoped we would get back together. Like there was a chance! By the second week, they stopped talking about it. Wendy was consumed with cheerleading, and Jenna was consumed with Matt. Every time Jenna said his name—which was several times a day—it secretly hurt that she had a boyfriend, and I didn't.

Walking home from school on a Friday in early May, I tried telling Jenna how sad I still felt, but before I even mentioned J.W. she asked, "Don't you have a Wacky Water shoot coming up?"

"On Monday," I said.

I was dreading it. The good news, which we'd told Eleanor, was that the medicine was working—the zits on my face and upper back were fading. The bad news we *didn't* mention was the red scars that remained, almost as noticeable as the pimples themselves. Eleanor wanted us to come to her office, but Mom firmly declined, using work as an excuse. We hoped another session at Totally Tan would even out my skin.

"Matt and I were talking about your acting last night," Jenna went on. "The whole TV commercial industry is so shallow. It's based on looking a certain way, and has nothing do with your value as a person. Who needs it?"

"I love acting." How many times did I have to say it? Why didn't Jenna or Dad understand? Yeah, reciting a few lines in commercials wouldn't win me an Oscar, but it was a start. Although, the truth was, the last play I'd been in was the sixth-grade holiday pageant. Maybe I was kidding myself to think I had any talent at all.

"So why don't you join the community theater or take a class or something?" Jenna suggested, as if I'd never thought of that and been talked out of it by Eleanor.

It's *my* life and my decisions to make—not Jenna's.

That's why I hadn't even talked to her about my acne treatment. I knew she'd just lecture me. And why were she and Matt discussing me when they could debate important issues like capital punishment and euthanasia?

"Who'd want to see me in a play right now?" I said. "Even Madison and Lily avoid me. At lunch, they barely say anything."

"They know you're sensitive about the acne," Jenna explained. "They're not sure what to say, especially since you barely talk. Anyway, I can tell your skin's getting better, O."

"But look what it's already screwed up. Wacky Water, J.W.—"

"—is a schmuck," Jenna said. "Even Matt says that, and they're friends."

Schmuck or not, I couldn't stop remembering J.W. waiting for me at my locker, kissing me in the park, holding me on the dance floor. He'd been my first real boyfriend. How could J.W. kiss me like that and then just blow me off?

"Olivia." Jenna stopped at her street corner. "You've got to get over him."

"I know that!" I cried. Jenna didn't understand how much it hurt to be dumped. She didn't have a clue about rejection because she'd never experienced it. She'd never even liked a guy until Matt. "Would you please do me a favor and stop acting like you're an expert on *everything*?"

"Excuse me for trying to help!" Jenna glared at me.

"Consider me *off* the case."

She turned and sped down the street, not looking back.

I stayed home, alone, all weekend. Mom was out showing houses, Aunt Barb was studying for cooking school finals, Wendy was at a cheerleading minicamp, Megan was at Cindy's . . . and Jenna didn't call. Or care. She was, no doubt, with Matt, telling him what an idiot I was. Well, I wasn't going to prove it by calling her.

Every hour brought me closer to the next Wacky Water shoot. Sunday afternoon Eleanor left two voice-mails, demanding a skin update before sundown. I didn't answer. Two cystic pimples had erupted on my face in the past forty-eight hours—from all the stress, I bet. Dr. T's office was closed for the weekend so I couldn't get cortisone shots, and I couldn't bring myself to tell Eleanor. Better to let Mom do it. Trying my best to relax, I did some yoga moves I learned at Kim's studio. I hadn't joined a yoga class yet, but I wanted to. I lay in bed for hours, pretending to be asleep when Megan peeked in, and didn't rise until Barb showed up early that evening.

"Dinner is served!" she yelled up the stairs. Mom was still at work.

In the dining room, Barb set out deli sandwiches, baked potato chips, and a Boston cream pie. Megan tore into a turkey on rye and slurped her apple juice. She'd given up on going vegan as soon as we left Albuquerque.

"Save room for some pie," Barb instructed.

I nodded, staring at my food.

"Why the long face?" Barb asked.

Megan answered for me. "Olivia's scared about going to Wacky Water tomorrow."

As immature as Megan can be sometimes, other times she totally gets it. We hadn't talked all day, yet after being around me for ten seconds, she *knew*. Sitting at the table in her purple nightgown, flushed pink from her bath, Megan was like a wise little Buddha.

My cell phone rang. Barb, who was sitting closest to it, saw the Caller ID and whistled. "Ex-boyfriend alert."

I nearly tripped over my pajama bottoms grabbing the phone and racing upstairs. I shut my bedroom door, dropped to the floor, and took several deep yoga breaths. J.W. *did* care. Otherwise, why else would he call now? "Hey . . ." I began, breathless.

"Olivia?"

It was a guy's voice, but softer—not J.W. "Who's this?" I asked.

"Theo."

Had J.W. put Theo up to some stupid prank call? Would Theo go along with that? "Why are you calling from J.W.'s cell?"

"I'm at his house for dinner," Theo said. "I forgot to bring mine."

"Is J.W. there?"

"He's playing basketball outside. I'm in his room, and I thought about you. I mean . . . I hadn't talked to you in a while. How, um, are you?"

Theo *had* to have heard how I was, from J.W. And here he was trying to be nice. I gave it to him straight. Why bother pretending? "Not so hot."

"Sorry, Olivia."

"I've been getting that a lot lately."

"My cousin's a dope," Theo said.

"Now you tell me," I cracked.

"I don't know what J.W.'s deal is, but I hope we're still friends."

"Me, too," I said. But I doubted we'd be running into each other much. When I started at Hillside High in September, he'd be a sophomore.

I heard a muffled voice in the background, asking Theo, *"Who are you talking to?"* Three seconds later, J.W. came on the line. "Olivia?"

My heart stopped. "Hey, J.W."

"Is Theo bothering you?" he teased. "I can put a stop to it."

Was everything a joke to him?

"We were having a *conversation*," I said coolly.

"Oh. Hey, I've been meaning to talk to you, too . . . since we haven't much, lately."

That was a major understatement.

"Life's pretty crazy, since I'm back playing tennis," he

said. "My week's jammed with practices and matches. You understand, right?"

I understood perfectly.

"Still friends?" he asked.

"I don't know," I said. I could have chewed him out, but J.W. wasn't worth it.

I hung up and dropped the phone—along with any hope that J.W. had ever really cared about me.

Monday morning came way too soon. Mom and I arrived at the Wacky Water set, both of us silent and tense. I didn't mention Eleanor's voicemails, and Mom didn't explain why she hadn't gotten home until after I was in bed. How could Mom have gone MIA again when I needed her? My body was bursting with stress, and pus-filled zits mingled with my scars. I was ready to give up.

Mom dropped me off at the entrance, and went to search for a parking space. I headed into the cast tent, assuming the usual position—head down. There were hordes of people, but no sign of Diane or Meadow. At the snack station, Kevin was noshing on a blueberry bagel. He choked at the sight of me. "Wh-o-a, Olivia. Um . . . Diane's looking for you."

"Olivia!" Diane called from behind us.

Once again, there was no escape. Diane swooped down on me like a vulture in black designer clothes.

"Come along," she ordered, charging ahead. "Eleanor is waiting."

Eleanor?

I trailed after Diane past the camera crew and extras, into a building with a small office. Where no one could hear me scream.

Then Eleanor and Mom entered the room.

They've got Mom, too, I thought, nervously giggling.

Eleanor wagged a plump finger at me. "There's nothing funny about this, young lady."

"Olivia," Diane began, "we discussed your skin problem at the last shoot. Do you remember?"

"I have acne, not amnesia."

"Olivia!" Mom scolded.

But I was angry now—at Mom. She'd spent most of the weekend working, barely checking in, like she was avoiding me. Or was she trying to avoid the whole situation? I had no idea what was going on in her head. And later today she was traveling to San Jose for a four-day work conference, leaving Barb to babysit Megan and me. The least she could do was be on my side.

Diane exhaled loudly. "I do sympathize, Olivia, but we're here to make a commercial. We lost valuable time with Kevin's injury. We can't lose anymore. I'm afraid we're at a dead end."

Diane was right. In the past three years, I hadn't once missed or messed up a commercial shoot—I left each job feeling that I'd given my all. But I had nothing to offer now. I couldn't fix this . . . and I didn't care anymore. I just wanted it to be over.

But Eleanor wouldn't let go. She snapped at Mom, "I called your home and cell yesterday. If you had returned my calls, we could have avoided this scene entirely."

"Olivia's done exactly as you requested," Mom replied. "She's being treated by your niece and following a strict regimen. Her skin *is* improving. Can't the makeup artist make her look alright?"

"No." Diane shook her head. "I'm afraid this is over. We chose a backup replacement for Olivia's role, just in case. The new girl's here, ready to shoot. We're canceling Olivia's contract. I truly regret that it's come to this, but as I said—"

"It's business," I stated flatly. "I wouldn't use me, either."

Not waiting for a reaction, I fled the office, the building, and Wacky Water.

But I had no idea where Mom had parked and the lot was enormous, so I sat on the curb for fifteen minutes until she showed up, saying, "Let's go home."

In the car, Mom sat, motionless. "What was that about? You acted like you wanted to be let go, Olivia."

"I didn't want to deal with it anymore, Mom."

"I can't believe the callous way they treated you!" Mom banged the steering wheel. "You've always done such a good job for Eleanor."

"Not this time."

She wasn't listening. "I know you love acting, and I don't want anyone ruining it for you. You're so lucky to have a calling, Olivia. Most people don't."

Mom was referring to herself, clearly. I think she's obsessed about succeeding because she hasn't—not professionally, anyway. Mom's always been more enthusiastic about my "career" than her own. But my commercial days were on hold—perhaps forever—and she didn't get it.

"My talent was being pretty, Mom," I said sadly. "And I'm not anymore. So I quit."

"You think looks are all there was to it?" She stared at me. "After all the time and effort you've put into acting, you're going to give it up, just like that?"

"Are you kidding me, Mom? I swear it's like you want me to be in commercials so *you* can feel good about it! Why don't you get a life and stop living through me?"

The words flooded out before I could stop them, but I meant what I said, and we both knew it. Tears trickled down Mom's cheeks. I had never seen her cry—not even once during the divorce. But she was now, thanks to me.

"Mom?"

She didn't answer. She turned the key in the ignition and started to drive.

Chapter Eighteen

PARTY ON

I didn't tell a soul about Wacky Water. It wasn't hard keeping it to myself. Jenna and I hadn't spoken since our fight, and we sat at opposite ends of the lunch table. We'd had minor squabbles before, but nothing like this. Wendy, Madison, and Lily weren't overly friendly, either. They looked at me, and looked away. They weren't the only ones. Other kids stared, and a few snickered. Were people afraid my acne would rub off on them? Or, like Jenna had said, were they just not sure what to say? Whatever it was, I felt completely alone.

Friday morning walking to science class, I saw J.W., Ed, and Wendy at the end of the hall, splashing each other from the water fountain. J.W. was in his blue rugby shirt and cargo pants—the same outfit he'd worn the night he kissed me in the park. Except now he stood close to Wendy—all smiles in her snug cheerleading uniform—holding her arms back as Ed sprayed her with water. Where was a teacher with a detention pass when you needed one?

Catching sight of me, Ed roared, "Hey, Zitface!"

People in the hall tittered. I cringed.

"Hey." J.W. sucker-punched Ed.

Wendy rushed toward me with a guilty expression. "Hi, cutie! I'm having breakfast at my house tomorrow before the class carnival. Wanna come?"

The PTA was hosting its annual eighth-grade class carnival for students and friends tomorrow, but I didn't feel like celebrating.

"No thanks," I said.

"Theo's coming," Wendy added, as if that might sway me. "And J.W. and Jenna and Matt."

"So?" My annoyance was gathering steam. They'd planned an event without even telling me? And why was Wendy having a water fight with J.W. when she knew how he'd crushed me? I've never flirted with any boy she's liked, and she's liked quite a few!

"I just thought . . ." Wendy hesitated. "Well, if you change your mind—"

"I won't."

Barb, Megan, and I watched *The Sisterhood of the Traveling Pants* Friday night, which I'd never seen. It was good, but I kept thinking, *Sisterhood, right!* Jenna wasn't talking to me, and Wendy was turning into a big, fat traitor. Did she like J.W., and did he like her? My gut instinct was yes to both.

By the movie's end, Megan was snoozing on the couch while Barb stove-popped a second bag of popcorn for us. I could inhale a gallon of popcorn and still eat more.

"Your mom should be home any minute," Barb said, carefully repositioning Megan so she could sit closer.

"She won't be psyched to see me."

"Sure she will!" Barb said. "She can't wait to get home to you and Megan."

Megan, not me. Megan doesn't say cruel things that make her cry. I'd told Mom to get a life, and there weren't many insults worse than that. When she called the first night from San Jose and I immediately apologized, she cut me off, saying, "*Let's just forget it.*" But I couldn't.

"I wasn't nice to Mom the day she left," I said, too ashamed to repeat the exact words. "I basically said she cares too much about my being on TV."

Barb crunched her popcorn. "I agree, but your mom just wants you to get what *you* want. She's protective, and worried that if you give up acting, you'll regret it later."

"Maybe I won't give up," I said. "But I need a break from Eleanor."

"Hear, hear!" Barb applauded. "I'm all for giving Eleanor the boot, right in the butt."

I laughed, picturing that. All the tension I'd been holding inside swooshed out of my body. I couldn't remember the last time I'd laughed like that. "Why is it so much easier to talk to you than to Mom?"

"Probably because I'm not your mom!" Barb said.

Ten minutes later, we heard Mom's keys rattling in the door. She came into the den, weighed down by her trench coat, handbag, rolling suitcase, and laptop. Dumping them all on the hardwood floor, she cried, *"I'm b-a-a-ck!"* sounding cheerier than I'd expected.

"Welcome home, sis." Barb rose from the sofa, lifting the empty popcorn bowl. "I'm going to fill this sucker up one more time. In the meanwhile, why don't you two kids make up?" She sauntered out, whistling.

Mom planted a kiss on Megan's cheek—Megan hadn't stirred in the last two hours. Once she's out, she's out. Then Mom knelt beside me.

"So how mad are you?" I asked.

"I'm not." Mom smoothed my hair back. "I've had a lot of time to think this week. The first thing I want to say is that I'm sorry about what happened at Wacky Water. I should have handled things differently, Olivia. I should have supported you and told Eleanor off. I've been so worried about you lately, but I was afraid if I showed it, you'd only feel worse. So I acted distant, which was really stupid. Can you forgive me?"

"I've been the one acting like a brat!"

Mom shook her head. "You've been going through a rough time. You always enjoyed making commercials, but

there's been nothing fun about Wacky Water, lately. I'm so
relieved it's over."

"You are?"

"I am," she said emphatically. "And you're right—I *do*
need to get a life. It's time to focus on what *I* want, and
let you decide what *you* want. I'm going to make some
changes."

"Like what?"

Mom grinned mischievously. "Give me a week or
two. But there's something I should tell you now: Eleanor
called. She has officially suspended you from the agency,
which she claims to feel horrible about, and says she'll
be more than happy to reevaluate things when you
'recover.'"

In one month I'd been dumped, fired, betrayed, and
now suspended. Yet this latest news didn't even faze me.
"What did you say?"

"That she can keep waiting, because we're not coming
back."

"You *said* that?"

"Yep." Mom beamed like a little kid. "Eleanor's not
the only game in town. When and *if* you want, we'll
find another agent. And whatever acne treatment we
decide on, it won't come from anyone pressuring us. I
should have said that from the start. Sometimes I make
mistakes."

"Mom," I said, hugging her, "that makes two of us."

• • •

For the first time in a long time I slept soundly. Saturday morning, I lingered in bed, listening to birds chirping outside my window. Making up with Mom was a good start. What came next was up to me.

When I finally got up at ten a.m., the house was silent. Mom had left a note on the fridge saying she and Megan were swimming at the gym, so I had the place all to myself. I toasted whole-grain waffles, sprinkled them with blueberries, and poured myself a glass of chocolate soy milk. Then I sat at the kitchen table, deciding whether I had the guts to appear at the class carnival. I wasn't dying to see everybody, but I didn't want to hide anymore.

There was a knock at the front door. I wasn't expecting anyone. I padded over in my slippers and peered through the peephole. It was Theo. I opened the door wide. "Hi!"

"Hey!" he said back. "Did I wake you up?" Theo looked really cute in a faded navy T-shirt and shorts. The San Francisco Giants cap perched on his head was a nice touch. The last thing I noticed was his cane.

"No." I inched behind the door, covering my pink plaid pajamas. "I just finished breakfast."

"So you haven't been out then, huh? It's going to be a great day . . . seventy-five and sunny."

I figured Theo wasn't here to deliver a weather report. "What are you up to?" I asked. "And how'd you know where I live?"

He ran his hand through his wavy hair. "From Jenna. I saw her at Wendy's breakfast party, but it wasn't much fun."

"Why not?"

"For one, Wendy chews with her mouth wide open. And two: you weren't there."

"Yeah, since I'm such a blast to be around these days!" But it was nice to hear.

"You might be, if you tried." Theo pointed to the condo parking lot halfway down the block. A pretty brunette in a silver hatchback waved at me. "That's my sister, Thora. She got home yesterday for the summer. She's dropping me off at your school carnival, and I'd hate to go by myself."

Leaning against the doorway, I asked, "Why aren't you going with J.W. and the gang?"

He looked right at me. "I'd rather go with you."

I was suddenly nervous, but the good kind of nervous— the kind I hadn't felt for a while. And I wasn't going to ruin it.

"I'll go, on two conditions," I said. Pointing to my improving, but still slightly zitty face, I said, "You sure I won't embarrass you?"

"Not if I don't embarrass you." He waved his cane.

"Fair enough. Number two: Are you up for walking?" I didn't want Theo to suffer because of me.

"Yes, Mom," he kidded. "So . . . you gonna get dressed, or what?"

I changed into an ivory peasant blouse and jeans, brushed my teeth, dabbed on sunscreen and makeup, fluffed my hair, and was out the door in five minutes flat.

Driving us to Hillwood, Thora jabbered away. She'd just completed her freshman year at Duke University in North Carolina. "It's nice to be home," she said, "but college is *so* liberating. There are lots of cool people, and a ton of guys to date! I don't put up with jerks anymore."

I wondered if Theo had told her about J.W. and me.

"Take my cousin, J.W.," Thora continued. "I hear he was a real jerk to you."

Theo had.

"Thora thinks most guys are jerks," Theo explained.

She ignored him. "I love J.W. He's family. But he's not nearly as wonderful as my little bro." She gave Theo an affectionate glance.

Theo turned beet red.

"And I hear you're an actress!" Thora said to me.

"Kind of."

"I'm a theater major," she said proudly. "And I learned so much from the high school drama department. You *have* to get involved. Hillside puts on fantastic plays."

The thought of acting—*really* acting—was exciting. "Does it take up a lot of time?" I asked.

"Uh-huh," she said. "Lots of evening and weekend rehearsals, plus the actual shows. But it's a total blast, whether you're in the play or on the stage crew."

Well, I wouldn't be auditioning anytime soon. But

being in the drama club would almost certainly conflict with the Ambassador schedule next year. I hadn't thought about Ambassadors in a while. . . .

When we arrived at school, Thora called out, "Nice meeting ya, Olivia!" before taking off.

Waving back, I said, "I like your sister."

"She talks a lot," Theo said. "But she's okay."

We ventured onto the football field, where countless white tents and tables had been pitched, and a row of carnival booths stretched the full length of the grounds. Theo and I stood in the food line, loading our plates with hot dogs, carrot sticks, potato chips, and brownies. I was still staying off junk food—mostly chips and sweets—but I figured a little treat wouldn't kill me. At a table by ourselves, we quietly munched away. I would have been happy to stay like that, but then we saw Jenna, Matt, J.W., and Wendy walking toward us. J.W. and Wendy stood close together. Wendy jumped when she saw me.

"Hi, guys!" Jenna waved to Theo and me.

"You two came together?" Wendy laughed nervously. "Smooth move," she said to Theo.

Wendy doesn't know when to stop. I nodded at her and J.W. and said, "You, too."

"Girls, girls . . ." J.W. stepped forward, clearly amused. "We're all friends, right?"

Wrong, I thought. He was enjoying this scene too much.

"*I'm* glad we're all here," Matt said, his arm circling Jenna's waist.

"Me, too," Jenna said. She smiled at me. "I miss you, O."

"I miss you, too," I said softly. She squeezed my hand.

"What about me?" Wendy displayed her most winning smile.

I didn't answer. Not because I was trying to be rude, but because I didn't know what to say.

"Why don't we catch up with you guys after we eat?" Theo suggested.

"We can wait—" J.W. said, but Matt dragged him off by the arm. Jenna and Wendy followed, Wendy giving me a pained look.

Theo moved closer to me. "I thought seeing those two might make you gag," he said.

"So Wendy and J.W. *are* together!" Mixed emotions boiled inside me. I didn't want J.W., not after the way he'd treated me, but I hated the idea of them sneaking around behind my back.

"They hung out during spring break and he's called her some," Theo said. "Why? Do you still like him?"

I admired how Theo didn't hold back. He just said what he thought. "I really liked him in the beginning . . . but not now. He may be your cousin, but he's not too deep."

"Yeah." Theo laughed lightly. "I almost told you that, but I didn't want to cause trouble. J.W.'s loyal to his friends, but girlfriends, not so much."

"So I'm just one of many?"

"Hardly," Theo said shyly. He slid his hand in mine. I didn't pull away.

"I should tell *you* something . . ." I said.

"What? Do you ditch guys?"

"No, but I, um, got ditched. And I'm not talking about guys." The words stuck in my throat. "I'm not going to be in the Wacky Water commercials. They couldn't use me because of my acne."

Theo nodded. "I hate that place, anyway. The water's full of pee."

"Totally," I agreed, laughing.

He dropped the subject. "Wanna check out the game booths?"

"Definitely," I said.

We wandered past various carnival stands—a fortune-teller, face-painting, and bounce house—before catching up to the others at the water balloon toss. The carnival was emptying out and there was no one manning the booth, but Ed, Danny, Lily, and Madison were there, too. Ed saw me and shouted, "Hey, Zitface!"

Theo spun around. "What did you say?"

"I wasn't talking to you," Ed answered breezily. "I was talking to Zitface." He tossed a fat water balloon back and forth in his hands.

Then Theo did something that I would never, ever forget. He casually lifted his cane and whacked Ed in the thigh. Not hard, but enough to make him lose his balance and fall.

"What the—" Ed stood up and rubbed his leg with one hand. With the other, he lobbed the water balloon at Theo's chest. "Take that, cripple!"

"*Not* cool!" J.W. yelled, knocking Ed back down.

Jenna, Wendy, Lily, and Madison rushed to my side. Clutching my arm, Lily cried, "Guys fighting over you? Impressive!"

But one guy wasn't impressed. Principal Brenner, an ex-Marine with forearms as thick as logs, strolled over from the cotton candy stand, where he'd had a view of the whole thing. "This party's over, folks." Staring down at Ed, Theo, and J.W., he said, "You can all follow me."

Chapter Nineteen

GROUNDED

"Theo's my hero!" I gushed to Jenna. We were at her locker Monday morning before homeroom. "Too bad he's grounded for a week."

"Heroes do suffer," Jenna said. "But Theo got Ed good. Not that I'm condoning violence."

"Of course."

Jenna stuck out her tongue at me. I knew we were good. We'd spent all Sunday together, talking and talking until our voices were hoarse.

She fished her lucky charm bracelet from her purse and clasped it on my wrist.

"What's that for?" I asked. "My acting career's on hold."

Solemnly, she declared, "I want you to keep the

bracelet, O. Consider it my official apology. I hope you can forgive me for being an insensitive know-it-all."

"You were being honest," I said. "I just didn't want to hear it."

Jenna had fallen over herself apologizing for not being there for me after the Wacky Water firing. But it had been my fault, too, for being too proud to admit it. I still hadn't told anyone besides her and Theo. People would figure it out soon enough—the first commercial was supposed to air any day now. The only thing on my mind today was how Theo had gallantly defended my honor against Ed. Principal Brenner had called the boys' parents to pick them up, but Theo swore that his punishment was a small price to pay.

"J.W.'s grounded for a week, and Ed's grounded until graduation!" Jenna said, her green eyes gleaming. "Lily and Madison told Principal Brenner how Ed's been giving you a hard time, and he told Ed's parents."

"They did?"

"Yep. They're sorry they haven't made more of an effort to talk to you about everything."

"I backed off, too," I admitted.

"Well, you don't need to anymore," Jenna said gently. "And to kick off summer, I'm throwing a slumber party. Can you make it?"

"I'll check my calendar," I kidded.

"Should we include Wendy?"

We glanced down the hall, where she was planted

at J.W.'s side, gazing at him adoringly.

"She swears she's been fighting J.W. off," Jenna said. "I've wondered about those two ever since I saw them at the ice-cream shop during spring break."

So *that's* what Jenna hadn't wanted to tell me during that call in Dad's car! But it was ancient history, kind of. . . .

"I think Wendy's liked J.W. all long, even before I did," I said. "They do seem to go together." I could picture her sitting beside him at Slice of Heaven on St. Patrick's Day, completely focused on him the way she was now. I realized that the things I liked about Wendy—her playful goofiness and outgoing personality—were also the things that had drawn me to J.W. "I guess you can invite her."

"That's generous of you," Jenna replied.

"I'm not psyched," I said. "But I'm moving on to better things."

"Like Theo?"

"Let's just say I wouldn't mind double-dating with you and Matt sometime."

Jenna tweaked my nose. "I'd say your chances are good."

Right before the homeroom bell rang, the class grew quiet. Principal Brenner was standing in the doorway with Ed.

Ed plodded over to my desk, biting his lip.

"Sorry about what happened at the carnival," he said quietly, for once, so the whole world couldn't hear. "I shouldn't have called you or that Theo guy a name, even though *he* took the first shot. I was just playing around. I didn't mean to hurt your feelings or anything. Principal Brenner said we could all go to Ms. Hirsch's office and talk about it, if you want."

It wasn't the most heartfelt sentiment, but it was a big gesture for Ed, even if Principal Brenner was making him do it.

"No thanks," I said. "I accept your apology as long as you call me OLIVIA. No nicknames. *Ever.* Deal?"

"Deal."

We shook on it.

After homeroom, I went to the counseling suite alone and knocked on Ms. Hirsch's door.

"Olivia! Come in."

I stood stiffly in front of her desk. "Can I talk to you about something?"

"Sure. What's on your mind?" Ms. Hirsch closed the file on her computer, giving me her full attention.

"This is kind of late, but . . ." I tried to remember the line I'd rehearsed. "I'm afraid I won't be able to adequately fulfill the duties of a freshman Ambassador."

"Oh?" Ms. Hirsch sounded surprised.

"Being nominated was a big honor," I continued, "but I want to focus on acting next year."

"Making commercials?" she asked.

I shook my head. "I'm on a . . . break. But I'm joining

the Hillside drama club in the fall. I want to be involved in all the plays."

"That's an ambitious goal," Ms. Hirsch said. "But not everyone's in every play."

"There's also the stage crew," I said. "I can learn a lot on the production side, too. Either way, drama club is what I really want to do."

She smiled. "Sounds like you've thought this through."

"I have. Sorry I didn't tell you until now."

"No harm done," Ms. Hirsch assured me. "A runner-up will take your place. You obviously have a passion for acting, and I'm glad that you're pursuing a school activity. I appreciate your honesty, Olivia. I wish you all the best next year."

The rest of May was busy, in a good way. I didn't mind studying for finals, because Theo made a great study buddy. As soon as he was ungrounded, his sister started dropping him off some days after school. We studied for our separate tests, but quizzed each other and ate snacks side by side in the den. Mom, who was working more at home lately, stayed close in the kitchen and Megan sat on the stair landing, listening. I knew I liked Theo as more than a friend, but I was waiting for a definite sign from him.

I hadn't broken out in two weeks, but I still had scar damage. Makeup helped a lot with that part. If the acne didn't reappear, I would start seeing Dr. T for ultraviolet laser therapy soon, to erase the scarring. The acne might be permanently gone, or not. Either way, I wasn't going to let it rule my life.

The night before final exams began, the phone rang and I eagerly picked it up. Theo called every night now. But it was Dad.

"Ready for finals?" he asked. Since spring break, our conversations were polite, but guarded.

"Nah, I dropped out. Mom's decided to home-school me."

"WHAT?" Dad bellowed.

Next Christmas I'm getting Dad a sense of humor. I flopped on my bed. "*Kidding*. I've been studying my butt off."

"That's what I like to hear," he said, laughing a little. Then he grew serious. "Listen, honey . . . I talked to your mom last night, after you were asleep. She told me everything that happened with Wacky Water."

For weeks, I'd gone back and forth on whether to tell Dad that I'd gotten fired. In the end, I'd asked Mom to do it because I was afraid I'd lose it with Dad if he sounded the teensiest bit glad.

"I should have been more supportive," he said, "but I think you're much better off focusing on school, and not listening to that lunatic Eleanor. I'm sorry you had to go through all that. You can talk to me about anything, Olivia, and I promise not to lecture or judge."

"Will you testify to that?" I asked.

"Well . . ." He laughed again. "I'll *try* not to, anyway."

It was something.

"And on that note," he said, "we will talk more, very soon."

My antenna perked up. "What do you mean?"

"I'll fill you in when I see you at graduation," Dad replied. "Kim and I can't wait."

Friday morning, I finished my last test. I was done with science! For a few months, anyhow. The end-of-year bell rang at noon and I danced out of the classroom, proud of myself for studying hard and, I think, doing well. All that was left was to walk across a stage tomorrow and I was moving on to high school! Around me, papers flew and people cheered. Outside the school entrance, a jumble of eighth graders had gathered, everyone screaming, laughing, hugging, body-slamming, high-fiving, you name it. Wendy ran up and piled onto Jenna and me, yelling, "We're *don-n-n-ne!*"

"Woo-hoo!" Jenna hollered.

Wendy calmed down. "Can I talk to you for a sec, Olivia?"

"I can tell when I'm not wanted!" Jenna smiled and bounded over to a group of girls. She was as excited as I'd ever seen, since she and Matt would spend the summer together and get to see each other every day at school next year. So would Theo and I. I hoped.

"About J.W. and me," Wendy started.

"You mean John Wayne?"

"John Wayne?" Wendy echoed. "*That's* what J.W. stands for? Poor guy!"

I instantly regretted telling her, after promising J.W. that I wouldn't. But if Wendy liked J.W. half as much as I thought she did, hopefully she wouldn't blab it to anyone else. Quickly changing the subject, I said, "So you like him, huh?"

"Yeah," Wendy admitted. "I've tried *really* hard not to."

"Like, for months?"

"How did you know?"

I tapped my forehead. "Female intuition."

"Well, let me tell you, seeing J.W. like you instead was tough."

"Until I became Zitface."

"J.W. figured you needed to focus on your skin issues."

That was the lame line he'd fed her? And Wendy believed it? But as frustrated as I was with her, I wanted to put all this behind me.

"Did you ever consider just telling me that you liked J.W.?" I asked.

She took a deep breath. "No. I thought you'd be mad. But I'm so sorry if it screwed up our friendship."

Her lips twitched, like she might cry. Wendy's not used to apologizing. And I *did* understand not being able to resist J.W.'s charms.

"So . . ." Wendy gulped. "I really hope we're still friends?"

"Still friends," I said, as she moved in for a hug. I awkwardly patted Wendy's back. I couldn't say our friendship would be the same, but I wasn't ready to give up on her.

She let go of me, smiling radiantly. "I've even been researching acne, Olivia. So many celebrities have overcome it! Jessica Simpson, Avril Lavigne, Katy Perry . . . You're in good company."

Wendy always has a unique way of putting things. "Um, thanks," I said.

"I almost forgot, thank you so much for what you did!"

"What did I do?"

"You gave up being an Ambassador! I don't get why you did it, but Ms. Hirsch called me in after school yesterday. I was the runner-up!"

Oh, brother.

Chapter Twenty

STARTING OVER

Saturday morning was graduation. We weren't wearing caps and gowns, but the girls would be in dresses and the boys in suits. Mom and I had found a navy silk dress, sophisticated enough for a high school freshman. As we were about to leave for school, I took a last look in the mirror. My face wasn't one hundred percent clear, but I felt good.

Mom, Barb, Megan, and I arrived at the school stadium, making our way through a mob of students and families. The early June sun shone brightly, bringing the promise of summer. I waved to various friends, and then I spotted Theo talking to J.W. and Matt. He looked handsome in a dark-brown suit. I ran over and hugged him. Who says girls can't make the first move?

"Happy graduation, Olivia!" Theo held on to me.

"Aren't you two cute," Matt cooed. He wanted Theo and me to get together, according to Jenna.

"Lookin' good, Olivia." J.W. nodded. "When do we get to see you on TV?"

It was a fair question. I expected to see a Wacky Water commercial—without me in it—every time I turned on the TV, but so far, nothing. With Kevin getting hurt and me getting fired, maybe the ads had been delayed.

"Don't even go there, cuz," Theo lightly warned him.

"I just don't want to miss it!" J.W. flashed his trademark smile.

"Hey, John Wayne," I said, "give it a rest."

Theo and Matt burst out laughing. Of course they were in on *that* secret. They had lots of dirt on J.W., no doubt.

J.W. held his hands up in mock surrender. "Fine, fine."

"So . . ." I said with a smile, "see ya around."

"Trying to get rid of me, huh?" J.W. said.

"Yep," I said, and walked away.

Theo caught up to me, saying, "Guess you don't need me to defend you."

"Nope!" I agreed.

The school band struck up the music, signaling that the ceremony was about to begin. Theo pulled a small jewelry box from his coat pocket and handed it to me. "Just a little something."

It was my second real gift from a boy. Rich, last year's crush, gave me a stuffed bear for Valentine's Day, which I promptly passed on to Megan. I could tell Theo's gift was something special. Fingers trembling, I opened the box and saw a delicate silver necklace with a tiny, dangling peace symbol.

"I hope it's not cheesy," Theo said, blushing. "I just figured, the way things have been going, you could use a little peace. But . . . if you don't like it, I can take it back."

"Are you kidding?" I clutched the box to my chest, giggling. I stopped when Theo leaned in and softly kissed me on the cheek.

I turned my head, and he moved toward my lips, just as Megan ran up to us. Greeting Theo, she blurted out, "Where's your cane?"

"Megan!" I could have clobbered her.

But Theo didn't mind. "In my bedroom closet. I only use it to fight bad guys."

Megan laughed, twirling her skirt. She seemed to have a little crush on him. Not that I blamed her.

Mom and Barb caught up to us seconds later.

"Hi, Theo," Mom said. "Thanks for helping Olivia study for exams. Will we see you this summer?"

Theo coughed. "Sure, Mrs. Hughes."

"Have you seen Dad and Kim?" I asked her.

"Their plane got delayed due to thunderstorms," Mom said. "They won't make it in time for graduation. I *knew* he should have flown in last night."

"Easy, girl," Barb said.

"It's okay," I told Mom, and I meant it. I didn't feel an ounce of anger. I was sick and tired of feeling angry, and maybe Dad didn't deserve it. "I'll see them sometime today, right?"

Barb gave me a thumbs-up. "That's what I call mature thinking."

"We all have to grow up sometime," I said.

Post-ceremony, Mom treated us to lunch at a fancy French bistro. I ordered a walnut-Gorgonzola salad, chicken croissant, and a champagne cocktail, which Mom promptly nixed.

"You can taste mine." Barb passed her champagne flute to me.

"Hold it!" Mom said. "Olivia's *thirteen*."

"Almost fourteen," I reminded them.

"Ah, yes . . ." Barb sighed dramatically. "I remember my thirteenth summer well."

"I remember you spent most of it grounded," Mom said, before checking her voicemail for the tenth time.

"Dad and Kim still haven't landed?" I asked.

"Nothing yet. We'll have to toast without them." Mom set the phone down and raised her glass. "To my darling daughter Olivia, who's taught me a *lot* this year."

"To me!" I chugged some mineral water.

"We knew you'd survive middle school, one way or

another," Barb said. "Hope we can get Megan through it in one piece, too."

"Uh, thanks, Aunt Barb!" Megan said.

Mom covered my hand with hers. "Not to steal Olivia's thunder, but I have some good news to share."

I nodded at her eagerly.

"Here goes . . ." Mom took a gigantic breath. "I quit my job."

We all stared at her.

Megan dropped her spoon. "Are we going to be homeless?"

"No!" Mom shook her head vehemently. "Money won't be pouring in, but there will be a steady paycheck, which beats occasional commissions. I'm tired of working nights and weekends . . . and, let's face it, I stink at real estate."

Barb nearly spit out her food. "Are you drunk?"

Mom rolled her eyes. "Just happy. I met a local interior designer when I was at that conference in San Jose. I interviewed with her last week, and yesterday she called and offered me a job! I'll be an assistant at her firm, and she'll teach me the business. I've always regretted not pursuing my degree, and I finally have a chance to start over."

"*To starting over,*" I toasted her.

"And to my big sister, Linda," Barb added, "who can still surprise me!"

• • •

By the time we pulled up to our condo in the afternoon, all I wanted was a long nap. But the excitement wasn't over. Dad and Kim's rental car was parked in front, and they stood beside it with their suitcases. As soon as I stepped out of the minivan, they showered me with apologies as Mom and Kim exchanged awkward hellos.

"We're so sorry, Olivia," Kim exclaimed.

"I-I feel awful, honey," Dad said. "We thought we'd be here in plenty of time. We sat on the runway for *hours*."

Dad looked tense, waiting for my reaction. Sometimes, he's not so hard to understand.

"Don't worry about it," I said. "How long are you in town?"

Dad and Kim locked eyes and so did Mom and Barb, like they were all in on a big secret. Then Dad stood between Megan and me, with an arm around each of us, and announced, "I'm returning to the corporate office. Kim and I are moving to San Francisco."

"Ohmigod!" Megan shrieked, jumping up and down like she'd won the lottery. "I *knew* you'd come back, Dad!"

That made one of us. I was stunned.

"It was an easy decision," Dad said. "Because this is right where I should be—close to my girls."

Dad and Kim moving here would be a big change. But I had dealt with a lot of changes lately. I could handle this one.

"I'm glad, Dad," I said. "That's great news."

"The best!" Megan cried.

• • •

Sunday morning, Mom and I made French toast and fruit salad for breakfast while Megan slept in. We ate it out on our small backyard patio. It was a gorgeous June day, and the whole summer stretched out before me.

Sipping orange juice, I flipped through the Novato Community Theatre brochure. The class I'd signed up for—*Acting for the Not-So-Amateur*, an intermediate teen workshop for those with "previous acting experience"—started next week. Rereading the description, I felt a ripple of nerves. I'd wanted to take acting classes for so long, and I'd always let Eleanor talk me out of it. I wasn't even sure why. Maybe I'd been afraid to try something new. But not anymore. I'd even signed up for a yoga class at the local Y.

Mom settled onto the other lounge chair armed with coffee, a pencil, and *The New York Times* crossword puzzle. "So . . . how do you really feel about your dad's big news?"

"Pretty good. Maybe Dad and I can finally work things out."

"Spending more time together might help," she agreed. "I'm so glad he's moving back. Oh, and, speaking of news, someone called while you were sleeping."

"Jenna?"

"No."

"Theo?"

"Nope."

"Wendy?"

"Guess again."

"Dad?"

"Wrong!"

I gave up. "So who was it?"

"Eleanor."

I sat up. "What's *she* calling about?"

"You won't believe this—well, actually, you probably will—but Eleanor's assistant, Peter, attended your graduation yesterday."

"Huh?" That didn't make sense. "I didn't see Peter there."

"You weren't supposed to. I bet he stood in the back, with binoculars."

"I don't get it."

"Eleanor must have second thoughts about suspending you," Mom explained. "She called a few days ago, but I didn't answer. Maybe she thought I never would, because today she said she had Peter attend graduation to 'see how you are.' Apparently, the report was favorable."

I could *totally* see Eleanor making him do that. Until Wacky Water, she always said I was one of her best clients. If she thought I looked better, I could see her wanting me back.

"She wants us to come in and talk things over. . . ."

"Oh, boy."

"I said I'd have to check with you," Mom said. "What should I tell her?"

I sat there, thinking. I still thought Eleanor was a head case. That hadn't changed. And, for a second, I thought my life could go right back to the way it was, before acne . . . the past few months forgotten. But, then, I would still be under Eleanor's control. I would still like J.W., not Theo. And I wouldn't have learned all the things I did about Mom, Jenna, Wendy, and everyone else, including me. And, just maybe, Dad wouldn't be moving back if we hadn't fought during my trip, forcing us to get closer, literally. A lot had happened in my life this spring and most of it, I realized, was good. I didn't want to hit the reset button. I wanted to keep moving forward.

Sinking deeper into the comfy chaise lounge, I tilted my head toward the sun, and said, "Tell Eleanor, no thanks."

Author's Note

Throughout my teen years, I considered myself lucky that I never seriously "broke out." Then—bam—acne hit me hard after college. Even though I had supportive family and friends, having acne was painful, emotionally and physically. Acne can't always be concealed, even with the best cosmetic products. I often felt ashamed and embarrassed about my appearance, and sometimes avoided seeing people because of it. It was a distressing time, but it would have been worse had it occurred when I was thirteen. Early adolescence is a time of tremendous change, and *Zitface* reflects this. Acne affects every aspect of Olivia's life—romance, friendships, family life, and her acting career—turning her world upside down.

While *Zitface* is a work of fiction, teen acne is a common reality. Most teenagers—up to ninety percent, researchers say—experience mild, moderate, or severe acne. Acne isn't a life-threatening condition, but it comes with emotional side effects: typically, low self-esteem and depression. Getting acne isn't anyone's fault, yet teens who have it are often embarrassed and ashamed, and may go out of their way to avoid being seen—sound familiar? But "hiding" isn't an option at school.

There are numerous treatment options these days for acne (and post-acne scarring). However, as Olivia discovers in the story, there isn't usually a "quick fix" and the decision about whether to take medicine and which medicine to take can be a difficult one, for teens and their parents.

Thank you to Dr. Max F. Adler, M.D., of Park Cities Dermatology Center in Dallas, Texas, for his expert review of medical information.

Besides seeking treatment, it's important to have a supportive network of people who are understanding and available to listen. This may be family, friends, a school teacher or counselor, or perhaps a local support group. Acne isn't a problem you should have to face alone.